F
S        Simenon, G.          C 1

          Monsieur Monde
        vanishes

| | DATE DUE | |
|---|---|---|
| DEC 22 '84 | | |
| OCT 14 '89 | | |
| APR 07 '92 | | |
| | | |
| | | |
| | | |
| | | |
| | | |
| | | |
| | | |

RIC

# Monsieur
# Monde
# Vanishes

# Georges Simenon

 Translated from the French by Jean Stewart

A Helen and Kurt Wolff Book

Harcourt Brace Jovanovich

New York and London

# Monsieur
# Monde
# Vanishes

Printed in the United States of America

Library of Congress Cataloging in Publication Data

Simenon, Georges, 1903-
    Monsieur Monde vanishes.

    "A Helen and Kurt Wolff book."
    Translation of La fuite de Monsieur Monde.
    I.   Title.
PZ3.S5892Mm6   [PQ2637.I53]      843'.9'12      76-39800
ISBN 0-15-162098-9


First American edition

B C D E

*To* Professors Lian *and* Giroire

*and to* Doctor Eriau

*in memory of February 1944*

# Monsieur

# Monde

# Vanishes

# One

It was five o'clock in the afternoon, or a trifle after—
the minute hand was leaning slightly toward the
right—on January 16, when Madame Monde swept
into the waiting room at the police station, bringing
with her a gust of freezing air.

She must have jumped out of a taxi, or perhaps a
private car, darted like a shadow across the sidewalk of
Rue La Rochefoucauld, and stumbled, no doubt, on
the ill-lit staircase; and she had pushed open the door
so authoritatively that everyone had stared with surprise as the grimy gray panel, fitted with an automatic
closing device, swung slowly back behind her, its slow-
ness seeming absurd by contrast—so much so, indeed,
that one working-class woman, shawled and hatless,
who had been standing waiting for over an hour,
instinctively pushed forward one of the children clinging to her skirts with a muttered "Go and shut the
door."

Until Madame Monde's entry, the atmosphere had
been snug enough. On one side of the railing, clerks in
police uniform or plain clothes were writing or warming their hands at the stove; on the other side, some
people were sitting on a bench alongside the wall, and
others were standing. When anyone went out, carrying
a brand-new sheet of paper, the rest moved up one

place, the first clerk lifted his head. Everyone was resigned to the bad smell, the feeble light shed by two green-shaded lamps, the monotony of waiting and of filling in forms in purple ink; and no doubt if some unforeseeable catastrophe had cut off the police station, for any length of time, from the outside world, those who happened to be assembled there would have ended by living together like a tribe.

Without jostling anyone, the woman had made her way to the front row; she was dressed in black, and under the heavy powder her face looked very white and her nose had a mauvish tinge. Without seeing anyone, she groped in her handbag with black-gloved fingers like sticks of ebony, as precise in their movement as the beak of a bird of prey; and everyone was waiting, everyone was watching her as she thrust her visiting card across the railing.

"Will you please tell the Superintendent I wish to see him."

There was plenty of time to examine her in detail, and yet nobody formed more than a general impression.

"A kind of widow," the clerk told the Superintendent, who was sitting in his office amid a cloud of cigar smoke, having a friendly chat with the secretary general of the Théâtre de Paris.

"In a moment."

The clerk went back, and before resuming his seat and picking up the identity cards that were being held out to him he repeated the message:

"In a moment."

She remained standing. No doubt her two feet, in their trim shoes with inordinately high heels, were resting on the dirty floor; nonetheless she gave the impression of being perched on one leg, like a heron. She saw nobody. She stared icily down at nothing in particular, perhaps at the cinders that had rolled out of the stove, and her lips were quivering like those of old women at prayer in church.

A door opened. The Superintendent appeared.

"Madame? . . ."

He closed the door behind her, waved her to a chair upholstered in green cloth, then walked slowly around his Empire-style desk, with her visiting card in his hand, and sat down.

"Madame Monde?" he queried.

"Yes, Madame Monde. I live at 27b, Rue Ballu."

And she glared at the smoldering cigar butt which the Superintendent had crushed out in the ash tray.

"And what can I do for you?"

"I have come to let you know that my husband has disappeared."

"Very good . . . Excuse me. . . ."

He reached out for a writing pad and picked up a silver pencil.

"Your husband, you said? . . ."

"My husband disappeared three days ago."

"Three days . . . Then he's been missing since January 13."

"Yes; it was on the 13th that I saw him last."

She was wearing a black astrakhan coat that gave out a faint scent of violets, and her gloved fingers were twisting a flimsy handkerchief steeped in the same perfume.

"A sort of widow," the secretary had announced.

But she was not a widow, or at least she had certainly not been one on January 13, since at that date she still had a husband. Why did the Superintendent feel that she ought to have been one?

"Forgive me if I don't know Monsieur Monde, but I was only appointed to this district a few months ago."

He was waiting, ready to take notes.

"My husband is Norbert Monde. You have no doubt heard of the firm of Monde and Company, brokers and exporters, whose offices and warehouses are on Rue Montorgueil?"

He nodded, more from politeness than from conviction.

"My husband was born and has always lived in the house on Rue Ballu where we still live."

He nodded again.

"He was forty-eight years old. . . . I've just remembered: it was actually on his forty-eighth birthday that he disappeared. . . ."

"January 13 . . . And you've not the slightest idea? . . ."

No doubt the visitor's stiff bearing and tight-lipped air implied that she had not the slightest idea.

"I suppose you want us to investigate?"

Her contemptuous pout might mean that this was obvious or, on the other hand, that she did not care.

"So then . . . January 13 . . . You must forgive me for asking: had your husband any reason to attempt suicide?"

"None whatever."

"His financial position?"

"The firm of Monde, which was founded by his grandfather Antonin Monde in 1843, is one of the soundest in Paris."

"Your husband did not speculate or gamble?"

On the mantelpiece, behind the Superintendent, there stood a black marble clock that had permanently stopped at five minutes past twelve. Why did this always suggest twelve midnight rather than twelve noon? The fact is that one always thought of five minutes past midnight when one looked at it. Beside it there stood a noisy alarm clock that told the right time. It was right in front of Madame Monde's eyes, yet she kept twisting her long thin neck to look at the time on a tiny watch that she wore fastened to her dress, like a locket.

"If we rule out money worries . . . I suppose, madame, your husband hadn't any personal problems? . . . I'm sorry to be so persistent."

"My husband hadn't a mistress, if that's what you mean."

He dared not ask her if she herself had a lover. It was too improbable.

"His health?"

"He's never been ill in his life."

"Good . . . Very good . . . Right . . . Will you tell me what were your husband's movements that day, January 13?"

"He got up at seven as usual. He has always gone to bed and risen early."

"Excuse me; do you share the same bedroom?"

A curt, unfriendly "Yes."

"He got up at seven and went to his bathroom, where in spite of . . . never mind . . . where he smoked his first cigarette. Then he went downstairs."

"You were still in bed?"

The same stony "Yes."

"Did he speak to you?"

"He said good-by as he always does."

"Did you remember then that it was his birthday?"

"No."

"He went downstairs, you said . . ."

"And had breakfast in his study. It's a room that he never uses for work, but which he's fond of. The big bay window has stained glass in it. The furniture is more or less Gothic."

She must have disliked stained-glass windows and Gothic furniture, or perhaps she'd had other plans for the use of that room which her husband had insisted on keeping as a study.

"Have you many servants?"

"A concierge and his wife; she does the rough work and he acts as butler. We have a cook and a housemaid as well. I don't include Joseph the chauffeur, who is married and lives out. I usually get up at nine, after I have given Rosalie the orders for the day. . . . Rosalie is my maid . . . She was with me before my marriage. . . . I mean before my second marriage. . . ."

"So Monsieur Monde was your second husband?"

"I was first married to Lucien Grandpré, who was killed fourteen years ago in a motor accident. . . . Every year he used to compete, as an amateur, in the twenty-four-hour race at Le Mans. . . ."

In the waiting room, the people sitting on the greasy bench moved up one place from time to time, and others slipped out humbly, barely opening the door.

"In short, everything was just as usual that morning?"

"Just as usual. I heard the car start off about half past eight to drive my husband to Rue Montorgueil. He liked to read his mail himself and that's why he went to the office so early. His son left a quarter of an hour after him."

"Your husband had a son by a first marriage?"

"We each had one. He has a married daughter, too. She and her husband lived with us for a while, but now they're living on Quai de Passy."

"Good . . . very good . . . Did your husband actually go to his office?"

"Yes."

"Did he come home for lunch?"

"He nearly always lunched in a restaurant close to Les Halles, not far from his office."

"When did you begin to feel anxious?"

"That evening, about eight o'clock."

"In short, you've not seen him again since the morning of January 13?"

"I called him up soon after three to ask him to send Joseph along with the car, as I had to go out."

"Did he sound his usual self when he spoke to you over the telephone?"

"Absolutely."

"He didn't tell you he would be late, or mention the possibility of a journey?"

"No."

"He just failed to come home to dinner at eight o'clock? Is that right?"

"That's right."

"And since then he's given no sign of life. I suppose they've seen nothing of him in the office either?"

"No."

"And what time did he leave Rue Montorgueil?"

"About six. He never told me, but I knew that instead of coming straight home he used to stop at the Cintra, a café on Rue Montmartre, for a drink."

"Did he go there that evening?"

With dignity: "I have no idea."

"May I ask you, madame, why you have waited three whole days before coming to inform us of Monsieur Monde's disappearance?"

"I kept hoping he would come back."

"Was he likely to go off like this?"

"It never happened before."

"Did he never have to go off into the provinces suddenly on business?"

"Never."

"And yet you went on waiting for him for three days?"

Without replying, she stared at him with her little black eyes.

"I suppose you informed his daughter, who, you tell me, is married and lives on Quai de Passy?"

"She came to the house herself and behaved in such a way that I had to throw her out."

"You don't get on with your stepdaughter?"

"We never see one another. At least, not for the last two years."

"But your husband still saw her?"

"She used to hunt him out in his office when she needed money."

"If I understand you correctly, your stepdaughter recently needed money and went to Rue Montorgueil to ask her father for some. I suppose he usually gave it to her?"

"Yes."

"And there she learned that Monsieur Monde had not reappeared."

"Probably."

"And then she rushed off to Rue Ballu."

"Where she tried to get into the study and search the drawers."

"Have you any idea what she wanted to find?"

Silence.

"In short, supposing Monsieur Monde should be dead, which seems to me unlikely . . ."

"Why?"

". . . unlikely, the question would arise whether he had left a will. What were the terms of your marriage?"

"Separate maintenance. I have an income of my own and some property on Avenue de Villiers. . . ."

"What is your stepson's opinion about his father's disappearance?"

"He hasn't got one."

"Is he still on Rue Ballu?"

"Yes."

"Did your husband make any arrangements before he left? About his business affairs, for instance. I suppose these require some working capital. . . ."

"The cashier, Monsieur Lorisse, has his signature. . . ."

"Did the cashier find the usual sums in the bank?"

"No. That's the point. On January 13, just before six, my husband went to the bank."

"It must have been closed?"

"To the general public, yes. Not to him. The clerks work late, and he went in by the side door. He withdrew three hundred thousand francs, which he had had in his account."

"So that next day the cashier was in difficulties?"

"No, not next day. He had no important deal to put through that day. It was not until yesterday that he needed to pay out certain sums, and then he learned that the money had been withdrawn."

"If I understand correctly, your husband, when he disappeared, left no money either for his business or for yourself and his children?"

"That's not quite correct. The greater part of his capital, represented by various securities, is in his safe at the bank. Now he has withdrawn nothing from the safe lately, he has not even visited it, so the bank manager tells me. As for the key, it was in its usual place at home, in a small drawer in his desk."

"Have you power of attorney?"

"Yes."

"In that case . . ." he said, with unintentional off-handedness.

"I went to the bank. I had promised the cashier to let him have the money. I was refused access to the safe on the pretext that I could not certify that my spouse was still living, according to the accepted formula."

The Superintendent heaved a sigh, and nearly took a cigar out of his case. He had understood. He was in for it.

"So you want us to make an investigation?"

She merely stared at him once again, then rose, twisting her neck to look at the time.

A minute later she walked through the waiting room, where the woman in the shawl, leaning sideways under the weight of the baby she was carrying on her arm, was humbly explaining that for the last five days, ever since her husband had been arrested during a brawl, she had been penniless.

When Madame Monde had crossed the sidewalk, on

which the police-station lamp shed a red glow, and when Joseph the chauffeur had swiftly opened the door of the car and closed it behind her, she gave him the address of her lawyer, whom she had left an hour previously and who was expecting her return.

Everything she had told the Superintendent was true, but sometimes nothing is less true than the truth.

Monsieur Monde had wakened at seven o'clock in the morning; noiselessly, and without letting any cold air under the covers, he had slipped out of the bed where his wife lay motionless. This was his invariable habit. Each morning, he pretended to believe she was asleep. He avoided lighting the bedside lamp, and crept around the huge bed in the darkness, which was streaked by faint gleams of light filtering through the shutters; barefooted, holding his slippers in his hand. And yet he knew that if he glanced at the pillow he would see his wife's little black eyes gleaming.

Only when he reached the bathroom did he take a deep breath; he turned the bath on full and plugged in his electric razor.

He was a stout, or more precisely a corpulent, man. His scanty hair was fair, and in the morning, when it was ruffled, it gave his rosy face a childish look.

Even his blue eyes, all the time he watched himself in the glass while shaving, wore an expression of surprise that was like a child's. It was as if every morning, when he emerged from the ageless world of sleep, Monsieur Monde felt surprised to meet in his mirror a middle-aged man with wrinkled eyelids and a prominent nose topping a sandy toothbrush mustache.

Pouting at himself to stretch the skin under the razor, he invariably forgot the running bath water and would rush to the faucets just as the sound of the overflow betrayed him, through the door, to Madame Monde.

When he had finished shaving he would look at himself a little longer, complacently yet with a certain pang of regret because he was no longer the chubby, somewhat ingenuous young man he had once been, and could not get used to the idea of being already embarked on the downward slope of life.

That morning, in the bathroom, he had remembered that he was just forty-eight years old. That was all. He was forty-eight. Soon he would be fifty. He felt tired. In the warm water he stretched out his muscles as though to shake off the fatigue accumulated during all those years.

He was nearly dressed when the ringing of an alarm clock overhead told him that his son Alain was now about to get up.

He finished dressing. He was meticulous about his appearance. He liked his clothes to be uncreased and spotless, his linen soft and smooth, and sometimes on the street or in his office he would look down with satisfaction at his gleaming shoes.

He was forty-eight years old today. Would his wife remember? His son? His daughter? Nobody, most likely. Perhaps Monsieur Lorisse, his old cashier, who had been his father's cashier, would say to him solemnly: "Best wishes, Monsieur Norbert."

He had to go through the bedroom. He bent over his wife's forehead and brushed it with his lips.

"You won't be needing the car?"

"Not this morning. If I need it in the afternoon I'll call you at the office."

His house was a very odd one; as far as he was concerned, there was not another one like it in the world. When his grandfather had bought it, it had already had a number of owners. And each of them had altered it in some way, so that there was no longer any recognizable plan. Some doors had been blocked up, others put in in different places. Two rooms had been thrown into one, a floor had been raised, and a passage introduced with unexpected twists and even more unexpected steps on which visitors were apt to stumble, and on which Madame Monde herself still stumbled.

Even on the sunniest days the light in the house was dim and soft as the dust of time, and as though imbued with a fragrance that might have been insipid but that seemed sweet to one who had always known it.

Gas pipes still ran along the walls, and there were some burners on the back staircase, while in the attic lay dozens of kerosene lamps of every sort of date.

Some of the rooms had become Madame Monde's province. Alien, characterless pieces of furniture mingled with the old things that belonged to the house, and she had sometimes driven them out into the storeroom, but the study had remained intact, just as Norbert Monde had always known it, with its red, yellow, and blue stained-glass windows which lit up one after the other as the sun ran its course, and awakened bright little colored flames in every corner.

It was not Rosalie but the cook who brought up Monsieur Monde's breakfast, because of a strict timetable decreed by Madame Monde which determined where every member of the household had to be at various times of day. This was all to the good, for Monsieur Monde disliked Rosalie, who, despite the image her name suggested, was a gaunt and sickly girl who vented her spite on everyone except her mistress.

That morning, January 13, he read his papers while dipping croissants in his coffee. He heard Joseph opening the main gate to take out the car. He waited a little, staring at the ceiling as though he hoped his son might be ready to set off at the same time as himself, but this practically never happened.

When he went out it was freezing, and a pale winter sun was rising over Paris.

No thought of escape had as yet crossed Monsieur Monde's mind.

"Morning, Joseph."

"Morning, monsieur."

As a matter of fact, it started like an attack of flu. In the car he felt a shiver. He was very susceptible to head colds. Some winters they would hang on for weeks, and his pockets would be stuffed with wet handkerchiefs, which mortified him. Moreover, that morning he ached all over, perhaps from having slept in an awkward position, or was it a touch of indigestion due to last night's supper?

"I'm getting flu," he thought.

Then, just as they were crossing the Grands Boulevards, instead of automatically checking the time on the electric clock as he usually did, he raised his eyes and noticed the pink chimney pots outlined against a pale blue sky where a tiny white cloud was floating.

It reminded him of the sea. The harmony of blue and pink suddenly brought a breath of Mediterranean air to his mind, and he envied people who, at that time of year, lived in the South and wore white flannels.

The smell of Les Halles came to meet him. The car stopped in front of a porch over which was written in yellow letters: "Norbert Monde Corp., brokers and exporters, founded 1843."

Beyond the porch lay a former courtyard which had been covered over with a glass roof and looked like the concourse of a railway station. It was surrounded by raised platforms on which trucks were being loaded with cases and bundles. Warehousemen in blue overalls were pushing trolleys and greeted him as he went by: "Morning, Monsieur Norbert."

The offices stood in a row along one side, just as in a railway station, with glazed doors and a number over each of them.

"Morning, Monsieur Lorisse."

"Morning, Monsieur Norbert."

Was he going to wish him a happy birthday? No. He hadn't remembered it. And yet yesterday's page in the calendar had already been torn off. Monsieur Lorisse, who was sixty-six, was sorting letters without opening them and setting them out in little heaps in front of his employer.

The glass roof over the courtyard was yellow this morning. It never let the sunlight through because of the layer of dust that covered it, but on fine days it was yellow, almost pale yellow, though sometimes, in April for instance when a cloud suddenly hid the sun, it turned so dark that the lights had to be switched on.

The question of sunlight proved to be an important one that day. And then there was a complicated business about a flagrantly untrustworthy client from Smyrna, with whom they had been in litigation for the past six months or more and who always found a way to evade his obligations, so that although he was in the wrong they would end, out of sheer weariness, by allowing him to be in the right.

"Is the consignment for the 'Maison Bleue' of Bordeaux ready?"

"The truck will be leaving presently."

About twenty minutes past nine, when all the employees were at their posts, Monsieur Monde saw Alain come in and make his way to the Foreign Trade Department. Alain, although his son, did not come in to say good morning to him. It was like that every day. And yet every day it made Monsieur Monde unhappy.

Every day he felt like telling Alain: "You might at least look in at my office when you get here."

A sort of diffidence, of which he was ashamed, prevented him from doing so. Besides that his son would have misinterpreted such a suggestion as an attempt to keep a check on his punctuality, for he was invariably late. Heaven knows why; five minutes earlier, he could have gone with his father in the car.

Was it from a spirit of independence that he traveled to the office alone, by bus or by métro? And yet a year ago, when in view of his patent inability to pass his *bachot* he had been asked what he would like to do, he had replied of his own accord, "I'd like to join the business."

Not until ten or eleven o'clock would Monsieur Monde pay an apparently unpremeditated visit to the office of the Foreign Trade Department, and laying a casual hand on Alain's shoulder murmur: "Good morning, son."

"Good morning, father."

Alain was as delicate as a girl. He had a girl's long curling eyelashes, which fluttered like a butterfly's wings. His ties were always in pale pastel shades, and his father disliked the lace-edged handkerchiefs that adorned his jackets.

No, it wasn't flu. Monsieur Monde felt uncomfortable all over. At eleven his daughter called him up. There happened to be two important clients in his office.

"Excuse me, please."

And his daughter, at the end of the line: "Is that you? . . . I'm in town. . . . Can I call in at your office? . . . Right away, yes . . ."

He could not see her right away. He would have to spend at least an hour longer with his clients.

"No, this afternoon I can't. . . . I'll look in tomorrow morning. . . . It can wait."

Money, obviously! Again! Her husband was an architect. They had two children. They were always short of money. What on earth did they do with it?

"Tomorrow morning, right."

Well! She hadn't remembered his birthday either.

He went to lunch all by himself in a restaurant where his place was always reserved and where the waiters called him Monsieur Norbert. The sun was shining on the tablecloth and the carafe.

He caught sight of himself in the glass as the cloakroom attendant was handing him his heavy overcoat, and thought he looked older. The mirror must have been a poor one, for he always saw himself with a crooked nose.

"See you tomorrow, Monsieur Norbert."

Tomorrow . . . Why did the word remain so firmly fixed in his mind? The year before, at about this same date, he had felt tired, listless, ill at ease in his clothes, just as he was feeling now. He had mentioned it to his friend Boucard, who was a doctor and whom he frequently met at the Cintra.

"Are you sure there's no phosphate in your urine?"

He had taken a glass jar from the kitchen furtively,

without saying a word; he remembered it had held mustard. Next morning he had urinated into it and had seen a sort of fine white powder dancing in the yellow liquid.

"You ought to take a holiday, have a change. In the meantime, take this at night and in the morning. . . ."

Boucard had scribbled out a prescription. Monsieur Monde had never dared urinate into the glass again; he had thrown it out into the street, after deliberately breaking it so that nobody could think of using it. He knew that wasn't what was the matter with him.

Today, at three o'clock, feeling disinclined to work, he was standing in the courtyard on one of the plat-forms, vaguely watching the comings and goings of warehousemen and drivers. He heard the sound of voices in a tarpaulin-covered truck. Why did he listen? A man was saying:

"The boss's son is always after him, making proposi-tions. . . . Yesterday he brought him flowers. . . ."

Monsieur Monde felt himself turn quite white and stiffen from head to foot, and yet he had really learned nothing new. He had suspected the truth for some time. They were talking about his son and a sixteen-year-old assistant warehouseman who had been taken on three weeks before.

So it was true!

He went back to his office.

"Madame Monde wants you on the phone." She needed the car.

"Will you tell Joseph . . ."

From that moment on, he stopped thinking. There was no inner conflict, no decision to be reached, indeed nothing was ever decided at all. All that happened was that his face grew more expressionless. Monsieur Lorisse, who was working opposite him, glanced furtively at him several times and thought he was looking better than in the morning.

"Do you know, Monsieur Lorisse, that I'm forty-eight today?"

"Goodness, monsieur, I'm so sorry I forgot! I've had this Smyrna business on my mind. . . ."

"It doesn't matter, Monsieur Lorisse, it doesn't matter!"

He spoke more lightly than usual, as Monsieur Lorisse was later to remember, confiding to the chief warehouseman, who had been with the firm almost as long as himself: "It's funny. He seemed somehow detached from his worries."

At six o'clock he visited the bank and went into the manager's office, where he was welcomed as usual.

"Will you find out what I have in my checking account?"

There were three hundred and forty thousand odd francs to his credit. He signed a check for three hundred thousand and received the money in five-thousand-franc notes. He divided these among his various pockets.

"I could have them sent to you . . ." commented the assistant manager.

He understood later, or rather he thought he understood, for as a matter of fact Monsieur Monde was, even then, on the point of leaving the money behind, taking away only a few thousand-franc notes. Nobody ever guessed this

He thought of the securities in his safe. They were worth over a million.

"With that," he thought, "*they'll* be in the clear."

For he knew that the key was in his desk, that his wife knew where to find it, and that she had power of attorney.

His first idea had been to go off without any money. It seemed to him an act of cowardice to take any. It spoiled the whole thing. As he left the bank he felt ashamed of it, and nearly retraced his steps.

Then he decided to think no more about it. He began to walk along the streets. Occasionally he looked at himself in shopwindows. Near Boulevard Sébastopol he noticed a third-rate barbershop and went in, took his place in the line behind other customers, and, when his turn came to sit in the hinged chair, told the barber to shave off his mustache.

# TWO

He stared at himself in the glass, pouting like a child, and trying not to look at the other people but to concentrate on his own reflection. He felt that he was very different from the rest, that he had somehow betrayed them by coming among them. He almost wanted to apologize.

The barber's assistant, however, behaved toward him with indifference; he had merely given his colleague a wink as Monsieur Monde leaned back in the chair, but it had been a wink so brief, automatic, and unsmiling as to seem more like a sort of Masonic sign.

Was Monsieur Monde so very unlike the rest, with his sleek look, his expensive suit, his custom-made shoes? He thought so. He longed for the transformation to have taken place.

And meanwhile he was distressed because the assistant had a pink plaster on the nape of his neck, a bulging plaster which must conceal a horrid purplish boil. It distressed him, too, to see a tobacco-stained forefinger moving to and fro under his eyes, and to breathe the sickening smell of nicotine mingled with shaving soap. And yet there was something pleasurable about this slight pain!

He was still too new to it all. The transformation was not yet complete. He didn't want to look to the right or the left, in the chalk-scrawled mirror, at the row of men behind him, all reading sports papers and, from time to time, glancing unconcernedly at the occupants of the armchairs.

On the day of his First Communion, at the Lycée Stanislas, after he had walked gingerly back to his seat with downcast eyes, he had stayed motionless for a long time with his face buried in his hands, waiting for the promised transformation.

What was happening now was so much more essential! He could not possibly have explained it, or even thought about it in a logical way.

When, a short while before, he had decided . . . But he hadn't decided anything! He had had nothing to decide. What he was living through was not even a completely new experience. He must have dreamed about it often, or have thought about it so much that he felt he had done it all before.

He looked at himself, as the barber's fingers held his cheek taut, and he said to himself: "That's that! The die is cast!"

He felt no surprise. He had been expecting this for a long time, all his life long. But his nostrils were still unaccustomed to the cheap scents that he was now inhaling deeply; hitherto he had only caught a whiff of them as some workman in his Sunday best passed by. He was offended by the tobacco-stained finger, and the plaster, and the towel of dubious cleanliness around his neck.

He was the odd man out, the one who felt surprised,

for instance, to see ten people deep in the same sports papers; it was he who must seem strange, whom others would maybe point at?

If he had not yet experienced the ecstasy of release, it was because the transformation had barely begun. He was still too new to it, of course.

Once before he had got rid of that toothbrush mustache which had just been shaved off. It was a long time ago, two or three years after his second marriage. He had gone home, to Rue Ballu, in high spirits, feeling rejuvenated. His wife had looked at him with those little black eyes—they were hard eyes already—and had said: "What's come over you? You look indecent."

He did not look indecent, but he looked a different man. There was suddenly something ingenuous about his expression, owing to the pouting upper lip and the alternately pleading or sulky look of his whole mouth.

He paid and went out awkwardly, apologizing as he brushed against the crossed legs of those who were waiting.

Initiations are always painful, and this was an initiation. He dived into the street and began walking through districts he hardly knew. He was haunted by the feeling that everybody was watching him and he felt guilty; guilty, for instance, of having shaved off his mustache, like a criminal who's afraid of being recognized, and guilty, too, because of the three hundred thousand francs with which his pockets were bulging.

Suppose that policeman at the corner of the boulevard were to stop him and ask him . . .

He sought out the darkest, most mysterious streets, those where the lights reminded him somewhat of those of his youth.

Wasn't it extraordinary to be doing at the age of forty-eight, exactly forty-eight, what he had nearly done thirty years earlier, when he was eighteen? And to be feeling almost the same man, to such an extent that he never gave a thought to his wife or to his children, or to everything that had happened in between?

He remembered that first temptation very clearly. It had been a winter's evening, too. He was living on Rue Ballu—he had never lived anywhere else; but he'd had a room on the second floor then, over his father's study, the room that was now Alain's. The house was still lit by gas.

It must have been eleven at night. He had dined alone with his mother. She was an extremely gentle woman, with delicate features, a smooth skin, a melancholy smile. That evening she was paler than usual, with eyes reddened by tears, and around them the huge house seemed deserted. The servants trod noiselessly, and spoke in low voices, as people do in a house of mourning.

His father had not come home. That often happened. But why, at about five o'clock, had he sent the coachman to collect his suitcase and his fur-lined coat?

He had always had mistresses. For some time lately there had been one, a little actress whose picture was on all the walls of Paris, who seemed more dangerous than the rest.

He was an invariably good-humored man, always impeccably groomed; the barber called to shave him every morning, and afterward he would go off to fence at his club, and in the afternoons he was to be seen at the races, in a gray top hat and morning coat.

Had he gone for ever?

Norbert would have liked to comfort his mother.

"Go to bed," she told him with a somewhat mournful smile. "It's all right."

That evening he had stayed for a long while with his face pressed against the windowpane in his bedroom. He had turned off the gas. He was looking out. A fine drizzle was falling. Rue Ballu was deserted, and there were only two lights to be seen: a gas lamp fifty yards from the house, and the glowing rectangle of a blind in front of a window, a sort of luminous screen behind which a shadow passed from time to time.

Over by Rue Clichy life was flowing by; and Norbert Monde, his burning forehead pressed against the pane, felt a shiver run through him. Behind him there reigned a calm so deep, so absolute, that it frightened him. This house that was his home, these rooms that he knew so well, these things that he had always seen about him, seemed to be alive, with a menacing and terribly still life. The air itself was coming to life, becoming a threat.

It was a dark world, peopled with ghosts, that

enclosed him, seeking to hold him back at all costs, to prevent him from going elsewhere, from discovering another life.

Then a woman passed by. He could see only her black silhouette, with an umbrella. She was walking fast, holding up her skirt with one hand, over the wet gleaming sidewalk, she was about to turn the corner of the street, she had turned it, and he felt a longing to run, to get out of the house; it seemed to him that he could still do it, that one great effort would be enough, that once outside he would be saved.

He would rush forward, would plunge head foremost into that stream of life that was flowing all around the petrified house.

He gave a start because the door was opening noiselessly in the darkness. He was terrified, and he opened his mouth to scream, but a gentle voice said softly: "Are you asleep?"

That day, the choice had still been open to him. He had missed his opportunity.

He was to miss another, later, during his first marriage.

It was with a strange sense of pleasure mingled with dread that he thought about it, now that he had at last achieved what had been ordained from the beginning.

He had been thirty-two; in appearance, much like today, as stout or even stouter. At school his companions had nicknamed him Podge; and yet there was nothing flabby about him.

It was a Sunday. A winter Sunday once again, but as far as he could remember it was at the beginning of winter, which always seems gloomier because it suggests lingering autumn rather than approaching spring.

Why, on this occasion, was the house on Rue Ballu empty? The servants had gone out; obviously, because it was Sunday. But his wife, Thérèse, who looked so fragile and so innocent? Thérèse . . . well! . . .

The two children were ill. No; just the girl, who was five and had whooping cough. As for Alain, who was only one, he was going through a phase of bringing up whatever he drank.

Their mother had gone out, nonetheless. She had invented some excuse or other. In those days she seemed the picture of innocence, and nobody suspected.

In short, he was all alone. It wasn't quite dark yet. It was freezing. Not only the house but the whole of Paris seemed empty, with the occasional rumble of a car along the paved streets. The little girl was coughing. Sometimes he gave her a spoonful of cough syrup from a bottle that stood on the mantelpiece; he could still point out the exact spot.

The day before, that morning, just an hour previously, he had adored his wife and children.

Dusk was spreading through the house, ash-gray, and he forgot to put on the lights. He walked to and fro, always returning to the window with its floral-patterned lace curtains. That was still another sensation that he recalled with obsessive accuracy: the mesh of the lace between his forehead and the cold pane.

Suddenly, as he looked down into the street at the man in a greenish overcoat who was lighting the only gas lamp within his field of vision, he was seized by a sense of detachment from everything: his daughter had coughed and he had not turned around, the baby might have been vomiting in his cradle; he stared at the figure of the man going off, and felt himself as it were impelled forward, he had an irresistible longing to go off too, to go straight ahead.

To go somewhere!

He had even been downstairs into his study, for no apparent reason, perhaps with some thought of going away? He had stayed there motionless for a long while, as though dazed, in the same place, and he had given a start when the cook—the one who had been there before he was born, and who had since died—had exclaimed, with her hat still on her head and mittens on her frozen hands:

"Have you gone deaf? Don't you hear the child screaming his head off?"

And now he was in the street. He walked along, gazing with something akin to terror at the shadowy figures that brushed against him and at the endless tangle of dark streets, crammed with invisible life.

He had a meal somewhere near the Bastille—he remembered crossing Place des Vosges diagonally—in a little restaurant where there were paper napkins on the marble-top tables.

"Tomorrow!"

Then he went for a walk along the Seine. In this, again, he was involuntarily performing an old-established rite.

He still felt diffident and awkward. He was really too new to it. To do the thing properly, to carry it through, he ought to have gone down one of the flights of stone steps leading to the water's edge. Whenever he crossed the Seine in the morning he used to glance under the bridges, in order to revive another very ancient memory, dating from the days when he went to the Lycée Stanislas and would sometimes make his way there leisurely on foot: under the Pont Neuf he had caught sight of two old, or ageless, men, gray and shaggy as neglected statues; they were sitting on a heap of stones, and while one of them ate a sausage the other bandaged his feet with strips of cotton.

He did not know what time it was. He had not thought about it once since leaving the bank. The streets were emptying. Buses were becoming fewer. Then groups of people passed him talking very loudly, presumably on their way back from theaters or the movies.

His plan was to choose a third-rate hotel like the one he had noticed a short while before in a little street close to Place des Vosges. He still felt reluctant to do so, because of the way he was dressed and because of the three hundred thousand francs.

He found a modest but decent place near Boulevard Saint-Michel and went in. There was a smell of cooking. A night porter in slippers fiddled for a long time with the keys before handing him one.

"Fourth floor . . . the second door . . . Try not to make a noise."

For the first time, at forty-eight—as though he had made himself a present of it, on that birthday that everyone had forgotten!—he was a man all alone, but he was not yet a man in the street.

He was still concerned about giving offense, of seeming out of place. For it was not shyness. He was not embarrassed for his own sake, but he was afraid of embarrassing other people.

For ten minutes, at least, he had been prowling around the narrow house, which he had found without too much difficulty. The sun was shining; the butchers' and dairymen's shops were full of provisions which, exuding their mingled smells, overflowed onto the sidewalk, and it was difficult to make one's way through the bustling crowd of housewives and vendors in the street market of Rue de Buci.

From time to time, with an instinctive gesture of which he was ashamed, Monsieur Monde felt his pockets to make sure nobody had stolen his bank notes. In fact, how was he going to manage when he had to change clothes in front of someone?

The problem worried him for some time. Then he found a solution, but he needed paper and string.

Paper was easy enough. He merely had to buy a news-paper from the first newsstand he saw. Wasn't it rather odd to buy a whole ball of string in order to use only a scrap of it?

That was what he did. He walked about for a long time, through a district selling food exclusively, before he discovered a stationer's shop.

And he couldn't do it in public. He went into a bistro, ordered a coffee, and went down to the wash-room; this was in the cellar, next to the bottles, and the door did not shut. There was only a gray concrete hole in the ground and the space was so narrow that his shoulders touched the walls.

He made a parcel of the bank notes, tied it up securely, and threw the rest of the paper and string down the hole; when he pulled the chain the water spurted over his shoes and splashed his trousers.

He forgot to drink his cup of coffee. He was con-scious of looking like a criminal, and turned back to make sure that the proprietor was not staring after him.

He had to go into the narrow house with its blue-painted façade, on which was inscribed in large black letters: *Clothing for sale and hire.*

"Do you know what Joseph does with the clothes you give him?" his wife had remarked one day, in an aggressive tone. "He sells them in a shop on Rue de Buci. Since they're almost new when you give them to him . . ."

She was exaggerating. She always exaggerated. She hated seeing money spent.

"I don't see why, considering we pay him, and pay him well, far better than he deserves, we should give him this bonus. . . ."

He went in. A little man who must have been an Armenian received him without a trace of the surprise he had anticipated. And he said hesitantly:

"I would like a suit . . . something very simple, not showy. . . . I don't know if you see what I mean? . . ."

"Good quality, just the same?"

If he'd dared, he would have said: "A suit like everybody else's."

There were clothes hanging everywhere throughout the house, in every room, town suits, evening dress clothes particularly, riding habits, and even two policemen's uniforms.

"A darkish cloth, please . . . Not too new . . ."

He felt worried, shortly after, because he had put down his parcel in the first room and now had gone up to the second floor. Suppose someone stole it?

He was shown suits, but almost all of them were too narrow, or too long in the sleeves or in the leg. He was standing in his underwear in the middle of the room when a woman came in, the shopkeeper's wife, who had something to say to her husband but paid no attention to him.

Whatever must they take him for? Surely for a man who was trying to hide; for a thief, a bankrupt, a murderer! He felt wretched. It was the change-over that was painful. Afterward, in less than an hour, he would be free.

"Now here's a jacket that might have been made for you. Unfortunately, I don't know if I've got the trousers to go with it. No. But wait a minute . . . this gray pair . . ."

Monsieur Monde submitted, for he dared not argue. It was all rather better quality than he'd have liked. Dressed like this, he looked like a respectable clerk, a careful accountant.

"Would you like shoes and shirts too?"

He bought some. A small fiber suitcase of an ugly brown, also secondhand, was finally provided.

"Are you going to keep it on?"

"If you don't mind I should even like to leave you my other clothes. . . ."

He saw the Armenian glance at the tailor's label, and reflected that he had made a mistake. He was not afraid of being followed. The thought had not occurred to him. And yet it vexed him to leave this sort of trace behind.

When he emerged, his parcel was still in the first room. The shopkeeper handed it to him. Couldn't he guess from the feel of it that it contained bank notes?

It was ten o'clock. The time when . . . No, no. He didn't want to think about what he usually did at such or such a time. The jacket was rather tight over the shoulders. The overcoat was made of thinner cloth than his own, and this gave him a feeling of lightness.

Why did he go unhesitatingly to wait for a bus, at the corner of Boulevard Saint-Michel, that would take him to the Gare de Lyon? He had not thought about it beforehand; he had not said to himself that he would do this or that.

Once again, he was following a preordained plan, for which he was not responsible. Nor had he made any decision the day before. It all came from much further back, from the beginning of things.

Standing on the platform of the bus, he patted his pockets; he leaned forward to see his reflection in the window. He felt no surprise. But he was still waiting, as he had waited after his First Communion, for something he longed for, which was slow in coming.

It felt odd to be following the crowd through the main hall of the station, carrying only a small suitcase like so many other travelers, then to take his place in the line at the ticket office and, when his turn came, to say meekly: "Marseilles."

He was not asked which class. He was handed a mauve third-class ticket, which he examined with curiosity.

He kept on following the crowd. One merely had to drift along with it. He was pushed and jostled, suitcases were flung against his legs and a baby carriage shoved into his back, the loud-speaker shouted orders, train whistles blew, and he climbed like the rest into a third-class compartment where three soldiers already sat eating.

What embarrassed him chiefly was his parcel, which he had not thought of putting away in his suitcase. It is true that the suitcase was already full, but he opened it and packed the contents closer so as to set his mind at rest.

Was life beginning at last? He did not know. He was afraid to question himself. The smell in the compartment upset him, like the plaster and the stained forefinger of the barber's assistant, and when the train started he went out into the corridor.

A magnificent sight, magnificent and sordid, met his eyes: the soaring blocks of blackened houses between which the train was threading its way, with hundreds and thousands of windows open or closed, linen hanging out, aerials, a prodigious accumulation, in breadth and in height, of teeming lives, from which the train suddenly broke away after a glimpse of the last green-and-white bus in a street that already seemed like a highway.

After that, Monsieur Monde stopped thinking. The rhythm of the train took possession of him. It was like some music with a regular beat, the words for which were provided by scraps of phrases, memories, the passing images that met his eyes, a lonely cottage in the countryside where a stout woman was washing clothes, a stationmaster waving his red flag in a toy station, people passing ceaselessly by him on their way to the toilet, a child crying in the next compartment and one of the soldiers asleep in his corner, his mouth wide open in a ray of sunlight.

He did not know where he was going or what he would do. He had set off. Nothing lay behind him any more: nothing lay before him as yet. He was in space.

He felt hungry. Everyone was eating. At a station he bought some dry sandwiches and a bottle of beer.

At Lyons it was dark already. He nearly got off the train, without knowing why, tempted to plunge right away into the spangled darkness, but the train moved off again before he had time to make up his mind.

There were so many things within him that he must settle later, when he'd got used to it, when the train stopped, when he reached some destination at last.

He was not afraid. He had no regrets. In most of the compartments the lights had been put out. People had fallen asleep leaning against one another, mingling their smells and their breath.

He dared not, as yet. And despite his weariness he went on standing in the drafty corridor. He kept his eyes averted from the next coach, where red carpets could be glimpsed.

Avignon . . . He stared in amazement at the big clock, which said only nine o'clock. . . . From time to time he cast a glance into his compartment, where he had left his suitcase in the rack beside various odd bundles.

Marseilles . . .

He went on foot, very slowly, toward the harbor. The big brasseries of La Canebière were still open. He stared at them with a sort of amazement, particularly at the men whom he could see through the lighted windows, sitting around their tables, as though he found it strange that life still went on.

These people were at their usual tables, as on any other evening. They had been in no train. They had just finished playing cards or billiards, or talking politics, and they were calling the waiter, or else the waiter, who knew them all by name, was telling them that it was closing time.

Some of them were coming out already, lingering on the edge of the sidewalk to finish the conversation they had begun, shaking hands, going off in various directions, each of them toward his home, his wife, his bed.

Iron shutters clattered down over windows. In the Old Port district, too, the little bars were being closed.

He saw the water quite close to him, small boats packed close together and lifted by the gently breathing sea. Reflected lights stretched out, and somebody was rowing, yes, even at this hour somebody was rowing in the cool darkness of the dock, somebody who was not alone, for there was a sound of whispering voices. Lovers, perhaps, or else smugglers?

He turned up the collar of his overcoat, the overcoat that was still unfamiliar to him, the feel of which he could not recognize. He raised his head to look at the starry sky. A woman brushed up against him, saying something, and he moved quickly away, took a small street to the right, and caught sight of the lighted doorway of a hotel.

It was warm inside, even in the entrance hall. There was a mahogany reception desk and a formal-looking gentleman in black, who asked him:

"Are you alone?"

He was offered a pad of registration forms, and after a moment's hesitation he wrote down some name or other, the first that came into his mind.

"We still have one room vacant overlooking the Old Port."

The clerk picked up the little suitcase and Monsieur Monde felt ashamed. Surely the man must be surprised at the meagerness of his luggage?

"It's on the second floor. The elevator doesn't work at this time of night. . . . If you'll come this way . . ."

It was a comfortable room, with a small washroom beyond a glass partition. Over the mantelpiece there was a large mirror, and Monsieur Monde looked at himself in it, a long, serious look, shook his head, started to heave a sigh but suppressed it, and took off his somewhat tight-sleeved jacket, his tie, his shirt.

Then he inspected his lonely room and felt a slight regret, which he hardly dared admit to himself, for not having listened to the woman who had spoken to him a short while before, by the water's edge.

Finally he got into bed and pulled the blanket right up to his nose.

# Three

Tears were gushing from behind his closed eyelids, swelling them as they streamed forth. They were no ordinary tears. They gushed in a warm, endless flow from some deep spring, they gathered behind the barrier of his lashes and then poured freely down his cheeks, not in separate drops but in zigzagging rivulets like those that run down windowpanes on rainy days; and the patch of wetness beside his chin spread ever wider on his pillow.

Monsieur Monde could not have been asleep, could not have been dreaming, since he was conscious of a pillow and not of sand. And yet, in his thoughts, he was not lying in the bedroom of some hotel of which he did not even know the name. He was lucid, not with an everyday lucidity, the sort one finds acceptable, but on the contrary the sort of which one subsequently feels ashamed, perhaps because it confers on supposedly commonplace things the grandeur ascribed to them by poetry and religion.

What was streaming from his whole being, through his two eyes, was all the fatigue accumulated during forty-eight years, and if they were gentle tears, it was because now the ordeal was over.

He had given up. He had stopped struggling. He had hurried from far away—the train journey no longer existed, there was only a sense of endless flight—he had hurried here, toward the sea, which, vast and blue, more intensely alive than any human being, the soul of the earth, the soul of the world, was breathing peacefully close to him. For, in spite of the pillow, which was real enough but unimportant, he had ended his journey lying by the sea, he had collapsed beside it, exhausted and already pacified, he had lain down full length on warm golden sand, and there was nothing else in the universe but sea and sand, and himself speaking.

He was speaking without moving his lips, for which he had no need. He was telling of his infinite aching weariness, which was due not to his journey in a train but to his long journey as a man.

He was ageless now. He could let his lips quiver like a child's.

"Always, for as long as I can remember, I've had to make such efforts. . . ."

No need to go into details here, as when he complained of anything to his wife.

Hadn't the servants whispered among themselves, when he was a tiny boy, that he would never be able to walk because he was too fat? He had been bowlegged for quite a long time.

At school he used to stare intently, painfully, at the letters on the blackboard, and the teacher used to say: "You're daydreaming again!"

It may well have been true, for he usually ended by falling asleep, willy-nilly.

"It's pointless trying to make him study. . . ."

He remembered standing still in a corner of the playground at Stanislas, while all the others were running about, or sitting at his desk ignored by contemptuous teachers.

And yet, by dint of patience and fierce effort, he had passed his *bachot.*

Lord, how tired he was now! And why were the heaviest burdens laid on his shoulders, when he had done no harm to anyone?

His father, for instance, had never had to make the slightest effort. He played with life, with money, with women, he lived for his pleasure alone, and he was invariably lighthearted when he rose in the morning; his son had always seen him go by whistling to himself, his eye sparkling with the pleasure he had just enjoyed or that which he anticipated.

In this way he had squandered his wife's dowry, and his wife had borne him no grudge. He had almost ruined the business inherited from his father and grandfather, and it was his son who'd had to labor year after year to set it on its feet again.

In spite of it all, when this man had at last succumbed to illness, his family had rallied around him, and he'd enjoyed the devotion of a wife who had never uttered one word of reproach and had spent her life waiting for him.

The whole thing was so overwhelming, incommensurate with words, on the scale of the sea, the sand, and the sun. Monsieur Monde felt like a great caryatid released, at long last, from its burden. He did not complain. He did not recriminate. He bore no resentment against anyone. Only, for the first time, now that it was over, he let his weariness flow out, like streams of rainwater blurring the windowpane, and he felt his body grow warmer and more peaceful.

"Why have you treated me so harshly?" he longed to whisper in the sea's ear.

He had tried so hard to do the right thing! He had married so as to have a home and children, he had wanted to be a fruitful, not a sterile, tree; and one morning his wife had left him; he had found himself with a baby in one cot, a small girl in the other, without understanding, without knowing; he had been in despair, and those whom he questioned had smiled at his innocence; and finally, in forgotten drawers, he had discovered horrible drawings, obscene photographs, unspeakable things that had revealed to him the true nature of the woman he had thought so guileless.

In his heart of hearts he had borne her no resentment, he had pitied her for the demon she had inside her. And for the children's sake he had married again.

He stretched out his whole frame in deep relief, and the little shining waves came up to lick the sand by his side; perhaps one of them would soon reach him for a caress.

He had borne his burden as long as his strength had lasted. How horrible it all was! His wife, his daughter, his son . . . And then money! . . . His money or their money, he no longer knew, he no longer wanted to know. . . . What was the good, since it was over and done with, and now at last . . .

Somebody was walking about. Loud footsteps that seemed to go right through him, a floor reverberating cruelly, a door opening and shutting, an agonizing silence; he was aware of two people face to face, two people looking one another up and down, who were both on the very verge of tragedy.

"No!"

He passed his hand over his face, and his face was dry; he passed it over the pillow, without encountering the damp patch under his chin. His eyelids were smarting, but it was from fatigue, and perhaps, too, from the soot of the train; and the train was responsible, too, for the ache in his limbs.

Who had said "No"? He sat up, his eyes wide open, and saw a slender ray of light under a door, the door next to his in a Marseilles hotel whose name he had forgotten.

The man who had said "No" was striding back and forth on the other side of the wall. The catch of a suitcase clicked open.

"Jean!"

"I said no!"

"Please, Jean! Listen to me! Let me explain, at least. . . ."

"No!"

The words came from outside, from out of the night. The man's movements were quick and unhesitating. Probably he was taking his scattered belongings out of

the wardrobe and cramming them into the suitcase. . . . Probably the woman was clinging to him, for
there was a soft thud followed by a moan. He must
have pushed her away, and she had collapsed somewhere or other.

"Jean, listen to me. . . ."

She must have been frantic. For her, too, the petty
considerations of everyday life and conventional
behavior no longer existed.

"I'll explain. . . . I swear to you. . . ."

"Slut!"

"Yes, I'm a slut. . . . You're right. . . . But . . ."

"D'you want to wake up the whole hotel?"

"I don't care. . . . If there were a hundred people
here it wouldn't stop me from going on my knees to you
and begging you to forgive me, imploring you. . . ."

"Shut up. . . ."

"Jean!"

"Shut up, d'you hear?"

"I didn't do it on purpose, I promise you. . . ."

"Oh no! It was all my fault. . . ."

"I needed a breath of air. . . ."

"You needed a man, that's all. . . ."

"It's not true, Jean. . . . For three days I hadn't
stirred from this room, I'd been looking after you
like . . ."

"Like a mother, I suppose you're going to say, you
trollop."

"You were asleep, and I went out for a moment. . . ."

"To hell with you!"

"You won't go away, will you? . . . You're not going to leave me alone? . . . I'd rather you killed me. . . ."

"That's what I feel like doing. . . ."

"Well then, kill me. . . ."

"You're not worth it. . . . Let me go. . . . D'you hear?"

He must have pushed her away once again, she must have fallen onto the floor, there was a silence, then the voice, whose pathetic tone had already become monotonous, the plea that was almost a parody:

"Jeaaan!"

"Stop bleating my name. . . ."

"I can't go on living without you. . . ."

"Go to hell!"

"How can you talk like that! . . . How can you have forgotten already. . . ."

"Forgotten what? What you did for me or what I did for you? . . . Tell me that. . . . Or rather, hold your tongue. . . . Where are my shirts? Where the devil have you put my shirts?"

And just as, between the acts of a tragedy, the players resume their normal voices, she simply muttered: "I sent three to the laundry. The others are on the top shelf in the bathroom cupboard. . . ." Then, reverting to her former tone: "Jean . . ."

He did not try to vary his response: "To hell with you!"

"What are you going to do?"

"That's my own business."

"I swear, since I've known you I haven't let a man touch me. . . ."

"Except the one you were coming out of the dance hall with when I turned up . . ."

"I'd asked him to take me back here. . . . I was frightened. . . ."

He burst out laughing. "That's the best yet!"

"Don't laugh, Jean. . . . If you go away, you'll be sorry for it tomorrow. . . ."

"Is that a threat?"

He sounded threatening himself. More than threatening, for there was a loud thud—perhaps he had struck her—then another silence, and a moan:

"You haven't understood. . . . I'm the one who . . . Oh no, after all . . . I'd rather make an end to it right now. . . ."

"Please yourself."

Footsteps; a door closing. It was not the door into the hallway but probably the bathroom door. The sound of water pouring into a glass.

"What're you doing?"

She did not answer. He was panting, presumably as he tried to shut a suitcase that was too full. Then he walked around the room to make sure he had forgotten nothing.

"Good-by!" he shouted at last.

Immediately the door opened again and a terrified voice exclaimed:

"Jean . . . Jean . . . !"

"To hell with you!"

"One second, Jean . . . You can't refuse me that now. . . . Listen. . . ."

He was walking toward the door.

"Listen. . . . I'm going to die. . . ."

He went on walking. She was crawling on the floor. One could guess that she was crawling on the floor, on the grubby red carpet of the hotel bedroom; one could imagine her clinging to the man's trouser leg, and being kicked away.

"I swear . . . I swear . . . I swear . . ."

She was gasping, and only blurred syllables rose to her lips.

". . . that I've taken poison. . . ."

The door opened and slammed shut. Footsteps sounded along the corridor and then moved away down the stairs. From below there could be heard the faint sound of a conversation between the departing guest and the black-clad clerk at the reception desk.

Monsieur Monde was standing in the middle of his room, in the dark. He groped along the unfamiliar walls to find the switch, and was surprised to see himself in his shirt, barefooted. He moved close to the communicating door to listen, and heard nothing, not a sob, not a breath.

Then, resignedly, he picked up his trousers from the foot of the bed, trousers that did not seem to be his own. Having no bedroom slippers, he put on his shoes, leaving them unlaced.

He went out of his room noiselessly, hesitated in

front of the neighboring door, and then knocked timidly. No voice answered. His hand turned the doorknob, but he still dared not push it open.

At last he heard a barely perceptible sound, as though someone were choking and trying to inhale a little air.

He went in. The room was just like his own, just a little larger. The wardrobe was wide open, as was the bathroom door, and a woman was sitting on the floor, curiously hunched up, somewhat like a Chinese mandarin. Her bleached hair hung over her face. Her eyes were red, but dry. She was clasping both hands over her breast and staring blankly in front of her.

She did not seem surprised to see him. Yet she watched him come close without making a single movement or saying a word.

"What have you done?" he asked.

He didn't know what he must look like, with his trousers unfastened, his sparse hair ruffled on his head, as it was when he got up in the mornings, and his gaping shoes.

She gasped: "Close the door."

Then: "He's gone, hasn't he?"

And after a silence: "I know him; he won't come back. . . . How stupid it all is!"

She screamed out these last words with the frenzy she had shown earlier, raising her arms to heaven as though reproaching it for the idiocy of men.

"How stupid it all is!"

And she got up, leaning on her hands so that at one

point he saw her on all fours on the carpet. She was wearing a very short, tight-fitting dress of black silk from which emerged long legs clad in flesh-colored stockings. Her lipstick and mascara had run a little, making her look like a washed-out doll.

"What are you doing here?"

She could scarcely stand upright. She was weary. She was about to lie down on the bed, the coverlet of which had been turned down, but before doing so she looked suspiciously at the man who had come into her room.

"I heard . . ." he stammered. "I was afraid . . . Have you . . ."

She made a grimace, as a spasm of nausea seized her. And she whispered to herself: "I must try to be sick."

"You've taken something, haven't you?"

"Barbiturates . . ." She was walking to and fro, concerned with what was happening inside her, an anxious frown on her forehead. "I always kept some in my bag, because he slept badly. . . . Oh God!"

She clasped her hands, as though to wring them in renewed frenzy.

"I never can be sick! . . . Perhaps it's better so. . . . I thought when he knew I'd . . ."

She was frightened. Panic was visibly overwhelming her. And her terrified eyes eventually settled on the stranger, while she implored him:

"What am I to do? Tell me what I must do!"

"I'll send for a doctor. . . ."

"No, not that! . . . You don't know . . . That would

be the worst thing. . . . It would be enough to get him arrested, and he'd blame me again. . . ."

She could not keep still, she was walking ceaselessly to and fro in the confined space of the bedroom.

"What do you feel?"

"I don't know. . . . I'm frightened. . . . If only I could be sick. . . ."

He didn't know, either. The idea of leaving her and rushing off to a pharmacy to get an emetic did not occur to him, or rather it seemed too complicated.

"How many tablets have you taken?"

She flared up, infuriated by his uselessness and perhaps by the absurdity of his appearance.

"How should I know? What was left in the bottle . . . six or seven. . . . I'm cold. . . ."

She flung her coat over her shoulders and glanced at the door, as though tempted to go and seek help elsewhere.

"To think he left me . . ."

"Listen. I'm willing to try. . . . I did it once before, when my daughter had swallowed a . . ."

They were both equally incoherent, and to top it all, the people on the third floor, assuming that the original scene was still going on, banged on the floor to demand silence.

"Come here. . . . Open your mouth. . . . Let me . . ."

"You're hurting me."

"That's nothing. . . . Wait a minute. . . ."

He was looking for something with which to tickle

the back of her throat, and his inexperience was such that he almost used his own handkerchief. She had one in her hand, a tiny one screwed up into a tight ball, which he unfolded and rolled into a tapered twist.

"Oh, you're choking me. . . . Oh!"

He was obliged to hold her head in a firm grip, and was surprised at the slightness of her skull.

"Relax. . . . My daughter was just the same. . . . There! Just another minute . . . D'you feel it coming?"

Spasms shook her chest, and suddenly she vomited, without noticing that part of her vomit hit the stranger. Tears filled her eyes and prevented her from seeing. She was vomiting reddish stuff, and he held her by the shoulders, encouraging her like a child:

"There! . . . There! . . . You see you'll feel better. . . . Go on. . . . Don't hold it back. On the contrary, let yourself go. . . ."

She was looking at him through blurred eyes, like an animal that has had a bone removed from its throat.

"Does your stomach feel empty yet? . . . Let me try once more. . . . It'd be wiser . . ."

She shook her head. She went limp. He had to help her to the edge of the bed, where she lay down, her legs dangling, and now she was uttering little regular moans.

"If you promise not to move, to be very good, I'll go down to the office. They must have a gas ring or something or other to heat water. . . . You've got to drink something hot to wash out your stomach. . . ."

She nodded her willingness, but before leaving the room he went into the bathroom to make sure there were no pills left. She followed him with her gaze, anxiously wondering what he was doing. She was even more surprised when he rummaged in her handbag, which contained crumpled notes, powder and rouge.

He wasn't a thief, though. He put the bag down on the bedside table.

"Don't move. . . . I'll be back immediately."

And on the staircase, where he endeavored to make as little noise as possible, he smiled rather bitterly. Nobody had ever done as much as this for him! All his life, as far back as he could remember, it was he who'd had to help other people. He had often dreamed, in vain, of being ill so that somebody might bend over him with a gentle smile and relieve him, for a brief while, of the burden of his existence.

"Forgive me for bothering you"—he had always been exaggeratedly polite, through fear of giving offense— "my neighbor isn't feeling very well. Would you be kind enough to boil a little water for her? If you have any sort of tisane . . ."

"Come this way."

It was night. The whole hotel was asleep. Somewhere in the darkened city could be heard the heavy rumble of a passing cart, and from time to time the carter cracked his whip to waken the drowsy horse.

"Did you know them?" asked the clerk, who had

promptly realized that the people in Room 28 were involved.

"No."

"Wait a sec. . . . I'm looking for matches. . . ."

There was a percolator in a dingy, crowded closet that served as pantry, but the clerk lit a tiny gas ring, with that calm, rather mournful air common to those who live by night, always alone, while others are asleep.

"I was surprised to see him go. . . . He's been ill for the last few days. . . . She used to spend all day up in the bedroom with him. . . . She took his meals up herself. . . ."

Monsieur Monde found himself asking, to his own surprise: "Is he young?"

"Twenty-two, maybe . . . I'd have to look at his form. . . . This evening they went out one after the other, and she went first. . . . When they came in again an hour later, I could see there was going to be some nasty . . ." He ended with a coarse word.

"He's ditched her, hasn't he?"

The water was simmering already. The man looked through his tins, and eventually found some lime flowers for a tisane.

"If you'd like I'll take it up to her."

"I'll do it myself. . . ."

"Some sugar?"

"Perhaps . . . yes. . . Thank you."

"Nothing very high-class there, you know . . ."

He meant the girl, obviously. Why did he say that? Did he suspect Monsieur Monde of some ulterior motive?

"If you need anything else, don't hesitate to ask. I'm here until six in the morning."

And he went back to lean on his elbows on the mahogany counter, pulled out an open book from under it, and started reading again.

When Monsieur Monde returned to the bedroom with a teapot in his hand, the woman had fallen asleep, or was pretending to sleep. He felt embarrassed, because her dress was hitched up very high, showing part of her thigh above her stocking. He felt no desire, he had no secret thoughts.

"Mademoiselle . . ."

She barely raised her listless lids.

"You've got to drink this. . . . I'd even advise you, if you feel up to it, to bring some of it up again, for safety's sake, so as to clear out your stomach. . . ."

It worried him to see the misty, faraway look in her eyes. She did not stir. He raised her body and held the cup to her lips.

"Drink . . ."

"It's hot. . . ."

The syllables were blurred and indistinct, as if her tongue were too thick.

"Drink it anyway. . . ."

He forced her to, made her vomit once more, but this time she shook with painful hiccups for a long time and seemed to bear him a grudge for this additional suffering.

"We'll feel safer now. . . ."

Probably because she was choking, she passed one hand over her shoulder, slipped it under her dress, unfastened her brassière, and, in a gesture that was unfamiliar to him and that shocked him, managed to pull it off and throw it onto the floor.

"Lie down. . . . If you want to undress I'll go out for a moment."

She did not give him the chance, but with an air of complete indifference pulled her dress over her head, peeling it off her body like some superfluous skin. He had turned his face to the wall, but he caught sight of her nonetheless in the wardrobe mirror. Under her dress she wore nothing but narrow pink briefs and an even narrower garter belt. When she bent forward to remove her stockings, her little pointed breasts seemed to hang in space.

Next she removed the briefs; the elastic band had left a reddish mark on her skin. When she stood there naked (only a faint shadow darkened her belly between the thighs) she tiptoed, after a moment's hesitation, into the bathroom, where she behaved as if there had not been a man in the next room.

She came back wrapped in a faded blue dressing gown, and her eyes were still misty, her lips pursed with nausea.

"I feel ill . . ." she sighed as she lay down.

Then, as he tucked the bedclothes around her: "I'm fagged."

She fell asleep directly, curled up in a ball, her head right at the bottom of the pillow so that only her bleached hair could be seen. A few minutes later she was snoring, and Monsieur Monde crept noiselessly back to his room to put on his jacket and overcoat, for he had felt cold.

Not long after he had settled down in the armchair beside the bed he noticed light shining through the cracks in the Venetian blinds. Noises began, some in the hotel, others outside. Particularly outside, the sound of engines trying to start up, motorboat engines as he realized, for he heard the splash of oars in the water, and the boats in the Old Port knocking together; a factory whistle blew; sirens, in the distance, in the harbor where steamships and cargo boats lay, were moaning interminably.

He switched off the electric lamp that he had left burning, and the bright streaks of the Venetian blinds patterned the floor.

The sun was shining. He wanted to look. Standing at the window, he tried to peer between the slats of the shutters, but could make out only thin slivers of things, part of the trolley pole of a passing streetcar for instance, some pink and purple shells on a little cart.

The girl had stopped snoring. She had flung off the covers and now her cheeks were crimson, her lips puffed, her whole face distorted with suffering. The gleam of her skin counteracted the effect of her make-up, so that she no longer seemed the same woman; this was a far more human face, very youthful, very poor, and rather common. She must have been born in some shanty in the outskirts of the city; as a small child she probably sat, with bare bottom and running nose, on some stone doorstep, and later ran about the streets on her way back from the elementary school.

One after the other, the guests were leaving the hotel; cars were passing in the street, and all the bars must be open by now, while in the still-empty brasseries the waiters were sprinkling sawdust on the gray floors and polishing the windows.

He had time to wash and dress. He went into his own room, after making sure that his companion was still asleep. He drew up the blinds and flung the windows wide open, in spite of the tingling cold of the morning air, and he felt life come pouring in; he could see the blue water, white rocks in the distance, a boat with a red-ringed funnel putting out to sea, leaving a wake of incredible whiteness.

He had forgotten the immense sea, and the sand, and the sun, and the secrets he had whispered to them, and if a faint aftertaste of tears still lingered, he was ashamed of it.

Why had they given him a room without a bathroom, when he longed for clean water to stream over his body and purify it? Probably because of his clothes, those drab, badly cut clothes in which he now felt so ill at ease.

He had brought no razor, no soap, no toothbrush.

He rang. A page knocked at his door. He felt reluctant to entrust this errand to him, to give up the imminent realization of his dream.

"Will you go and buy me . . ." And while he waited for the return of the uniformed messenger, whom he could see hopping along the sidewalk, he looked at the sea, which was no longer last night's sea, which had become a harbor furrowed by motorboats and where fishermen were sinking their nets.

For a long time, dazzled by the morning light, he stared at the drawbridge, whose gigantic metal carcass blocked out the horizon and on which, from a distance, he could just make out minute human figures.

# Four

Monsieur Monde had waited, because it seemed to him impossible to do otherwise. From time to time he put his ear against the communicating door and then went back to his place beside the window; because of the biting cold, he had put on his overcoat and thrust his hands deep into the pockets.

At about ten o'clock it struck him that the noise from the town and the harbor would prevent him from hearing a call from the next room, and he regretfully closed the window. His heart was heavy then; he ruefully smiled as he looked at himself in the glass, wearing his overcoat, beside an unmade bed in a hotel bedroom where he didn't know what to do.

He ended by sitting on a chair as though in a waiting room, beside the communicating door, and (again as though in a waiting room) he indulged in speculations and forebodings, he counted to a hundred, then to a thousand, tossed coins to decide whether to stay there or not, until at last he gave a start, like a man suddenly awakened, for he must have dozed off. Somebody was walking, not with soft barefoot steps, but on high heels that made a sharp tapping sound.

He hurried around and knocked.

"Come in!"

She was fully dressed already, with a little red hat on her head, her handbag in her hands, and she was just about to go out. A few minutes later and he'd have missed her. She had spruced herself up as if nothing had happened, her make-up was spick and span with a strange mouth painted on, smaller than the real one, so that the pale pink of her own lips showed below it like an undergarment.

He stood awkwardly in the doorway, while after glancing sharply at him—as though to make sure he really was last night's visitor, whose face she could hardly remember—she hunted for her gloves.

"Are you feeling better?"

"I'm hungry," she said.

She found her gloves at last—they were red, like her hat—left the room, and showed no surprise at his following her down the stairs.

The hotel looked quite different. By daylight the lobby, which was also the entrance hall, seemed more luxurious. The reception clerk behind the mahogany counter was wearing a morning coat, the walls were covered with laminated wood paneling, there were green plants in the corners and a green-uniformed doorman outside the door.

"Taxi, *messieurs-dames?*"

The girl refused, while Monsieur Monde, without knowing why, avoided meeting the eyes of the reception clerk, although the latter did not know him. The fact was that Monsieur Monde was ill at ease in his skimpy clothes. He felt awkward. Perhaps he regretted the loss of his mustache?

Once on the sidewalk he walked on the left of his companion, who stepped out briskly, paying no attention to him yet showing no surprise at his presence. She turned left immediately, and they found themselves on the corner of La Canebière and the Old Port; she pushed open a glazed door and threaded her way between the tables of a restaurant with the ease of a regular customer.

Monsieur Monde followed. There were three floors of huge, wide-windowed rooms where people were eating, where hundreds of people were eating, packed close together, while between the tables, along the passages, up and down the stairs, ran waiters and waitresses bearing dishes of bouillabaisse or crayfish, plates of shellfish stacked in pyramids.

The sun poured in through the bay windows, which went right down to the floor like those in big stores, so that the whole room could be seen from outside. Everyone was eating. People stared at one another with blank or curious eyes. Sometimes someone would raise a hand, calling out impatiently: "Waiter!"

A strong odor of garlic, saffron, and shellfish assaulted one's senses. The dominant note was the red of the crayfish gleaming on the waiters' outstretched arms and on nearly every table, and whose slender empty shells lay piled on the plates of departing guests.

The young woman had found two places by a wall.

Monsieur Monde sat down opposite her. He immediately wondered what she was looking at so intensely behind his back and, on turning around, discovered a mirror in which she could see herself.

"I'm looking pale," she said. "Waiter!"

"Coming!" Running up, he thrust into their hands a huge mimeographed menu, scrawled over with red and violet ink. And she studied this menu with the utmost gravity.

"Waiter!"

"Madame?"

"Are the andouillettes good?"

Monsieur Monde raised his head. He had just made a discovery. If he had asked the same question, for instance, he was convinced that the waiter, any waiter on earth, would naturally have answered yes, thus doing his duty as waiter. Can one imagine a waiter telling his customers: "They're horrible! Don't!"?

The waiter was, in fact, saying "Yes" to the young woman, but not a meaningless "Yes." You could feel that he was telling her the truth, that he regarded her differently from the hundreds of customers thronging the three floors of the vast eating mill.

With her he was both respectful and familiar. He recognized somebody of his own sort. He congratulated her on her success. He did not want to do her a disservice. It was therefore necessary to understand the situation, and he turned to Monsieur Monde, sizing him up.

"If you'll allow me to advise you . . ."

He never lost contact with the girl. Between these two, imperceptible signs were enough. He seemed to be asking her: "Playing high?"

And as she remained impassive, he bent forward to point out certain dishes on the menu card.

"Shellfish, of course, to start with . . . It wouldn't be worth coming to Marseilles and not eating shell-fish. . . . D'you like sea urchins?"

He spoke with an exaggerated accent.

"And then some of our own bouillabaisse, with crayfish."

"I'll have crayfish by itself!" she interrupted. "Without mayonnaise. I'll make my own dressing."

"And an andouillette . . ."

"Do you have gherkins?"

"And what wine?"

Somewhere near Chaussée d'Antin, in Paris, there was a restaurant with some resemblance to this one, and there, from outside, you could see through the windows large numbers of people munching their food. Now, heaven knows why, Monsieur Monde had sometimes envied them, although he did not really know what for—perhaps for sitting there in a crowd, all more or less alike, side by side, feeling at ease in an atmosphere of facile glitter, of stimulating vulgarity.

The customers, for the most part, must be visitors from the country, or people of moderate means who had decided to treat themselves to a good meal. At the table next to theirs, in the full sunlight, there sat in state a huge middle-aged woman, whose fur coat made her look even vaster, wearing diamonds, real or fake, in her ears and on her fingers, giving her orders in a loud voice, drinking hard and laughing heartily, her companions being two youths who could hardly have been more than twenty.

"Were you following us?"

He gave a start. His companion, whose name he did not know, was looking sternly at him, with a stubborn frown, and there was such cold lucidity in her gaze that he reddened.

"You'd better tell me the truth. Do you belong to the police?"

"Me? I give you my word of honor . . ."

She believed him readily; she probably knew a policeman when she saw one. But she went on, nonetheless: "How did you happen to be there last night?"

And he explained volubly, as though to justify himself: "I'd just arrived from Paris. . . . I wasn't asleep. . . . I'd only just dozed off. . . . I heard . . ."

"What did you hear?"

He was too honest to lie. "Everything you said."

The waiter was covering their table with overlapping dishes of hors d'oeuvres and shellfish and bringing them white wine in a champagne bucket. So his unimpressive appearance had not discouraged the waiter; perhaps this was the sort of place where unpretentious people came to enjoy themselves.

"I've asked the chef to take special care with your

andouillette," the waiter whispered, leaning over toward the young woman.

She remarked, as she spooned out the pale pink granular flesh of a sea urchin: "You're married. . . ."

She was staring at his wedding ring, which it had not occurred to him to remove.

"That's all over," he said.

"Have you left your wife?"

"Yesterday . . ."

She pursed her lips contemptuously. "For how long?"

"For ever."

"That's what they always say. . . ."

"I assure you . . ."

And he blushed, realizing that he must be giving a misleading impression of boasting of his liberty, as though he intended to take advantage of it.

"It's not what you think. . . . It's more complicated. . . ."

"Yes . . . I know. . . ."

What did she know? She looked at him, then she looked at herself in the glass just as ruthlessly, then she turned to glance at the bejeweled woman and the two young men.

"You'd have done better perhaps to leave me alone," she sighed. "It'd all be over by now."

Nonetheless she went on meticulously shelling her crayfish with her lacquered fingernails.

"Are you from these parts?" he asked her.

She shrugged her shoulders. No woman would have asked such a stupid question.

"I'm from the North, from Lille. And you're from Paris yourself, aren't you? What's your line?"

She was examining his suit, his shirt, his tie. As he hesitated in some embarrassment before replying, she went on in an altered, almost threatening voice:

"You didn't run off with the cashbox, I hope?"

Before he had taken in the meaning of this challenge, she went on as though she was quite prepared to drop him flat: "Because I've had more than enough of *that*. . . ."

"I'm not an office worker."

"What are you?"

"I have private means."

She looked him up and down again. What did she find reassuring about her companion's appearance?

"Good . . ."

"Moderate private means."

She must have interpreted this as miserly, for she cast a peculiar glance at the table loaded with food and the bottle of expensive wine.

Monsieur Monde felt his head in a whirl. He had had nothing to drink, had barely touched his lips to his misted glass, and yet he felt drunk with all the dazzling light and the bustling crowds, with the red of the crayfish and the dizzy speed of the waiters rushing to and fro, and the din of all those conversations, of those possibly confidential remarks that people had to yell out to be heard above the noise of other voices and the clatter of plates and cutlery.

"I wonder where he's got to now. . . ."

And as, with naïve thoughtlessness, he asked who, she shrugged her shoulders; she had him sized up now.

"It'll be his loss more than mine. . . ."

She seemed to feel the need to talk about it. Not necessarily to him, but to anyone. She was mixing herself a vinaigrette on her plate, carefully proportioning the ingredients.

"Mayonnaise doesn't agree with me. I don't know why I shouldn't tell you the whole story, seeing what he's done. I crawled at his feet, which I've never done to any other man, and he kicked me here. . . . Look, you can still see the mark. . . ."

It was true. At close quarters, a slight swelling on the left side of her upper lip was visible under her make-up.

"Real trash, he was. . . . His mother sold vegetables in the street; she was still pushing her barrow, only a few years ago. . . . It wasn't as if I'd run after him! But I was quite happy as I was. . . . D'you know Lille?"

"I've been through it. . . ."

"You didn't go to the Boule Rouge? It's a little dive in a basement near the theater . . . The boss used to run a night club on Place Pigalle. . . . Fred, his name was. . . . They only have regulars there, a good class of people, who wouldn't want to be seen just anywhere. . . . Businessmen from Roubaix and Tour-

coing, you know the kind of thing. . . . There's dancing in the evenings, and floor shows. I started off there
as a dancer three years ago. . . ."

He would have liked to know her age, but dared not
ask her.

"Waiter. Will you bring me a clean glass? I've let
some crayfish drop in it."

While never losing the thread of her thoughts, she
kept glancing at herself in the mirror, and she even
seemed to be listening at the same time to the conversation between the lady in diamonds and her two companions.

"What d'you suppose they are?" she suddenly de-
manded.

"I don't know. They surely can't be her sons."

She burst out laughing. "Gigolos, I'd say! And she
hasn't known them long. Maybe nothing's happened
yet, for they're glaring at one another and they don't
know which of them is going to win. . . . Her, I mean.
. . . Well, I bet she owns a food store, a fish market or a
delicatessen, in some smart district where business is
good. . . . She's treating herself to a fortnight in the
South."

The waiter brought Monsieur Monde his steak. "The
andouillette'll be ready in a minute. . . . It's coming
along nicely. . . ."

And the young woman went on: "My real name is
Julie. I called myself Daisy when I danced. The gentlemen used to drop in for apéritifs too, and that was
the nicest time, because there weren't any tarts. We

were all pals together. You may not believe me, but most of them behaved ever so properly with me. They just came there to get a change from their offices and homes, don't you see?

"One of them, the nicest of the lot, a big fattish fellow, rather like you, was running after me for at least three months. . . . I knew what he was after but I wasn't in any hurry. . . . He came from Roubaix. . . . A well-known family, very wealthy . . . He was scared stiff of being seen going into or out of the club, and he always sent the busboy to make sure nobody was passing in the street. . . .

"He wanted me to give up dancing. He rented a nice apartment for me on a quiet street with nothing but new houses. . . . And it'd all be going on still if it hadn't been for Jean. . . . When he came to see me he brought things to eat, the best he could find, crayfish ten times the size of these, pineapples, early strawberries in little boxes lined with cotton wool, champagne. . . . We had little supper parties together. . . ."

And suddenly, in an altered tone: "What did I tell you?"

He failed to understand. She glanced meaningly at the neighboring table and, leaning forward, whispered:

"Talking to the waiter about fish, she's just told him that if she had the face to sell it at such a price . . . I was right! She's a fishmonger! . . . As for the two kids, chances are they'll be scratching one another's faces like a couple of cats before the day's out. . . .

"Where had I got to? Just to make you understand that I'm not indebted to that Jean for anything . . . On the contrary! From time to time I used to go back to the Boule Rouge, as a guest . . . because I had good friends there. . . . But I was respectable. . . . If I say so, you can believe me. . . .

"That was where I met Jean. . . . He was just a clerk in a hardware store, but at first he tried to make believe he was something high-class. . . . Everything he earned went on his clothes and on drink. . . . You couldn't even call him good-looking.

"All the same I fell for him, and that was my bad luck. . . . I don't know how it happened. . . . In the beginning he used to threaten to kill himself if I didn't do what he wanted, and he was always making scenes.

"He was so jealous that I never dared go out. . . . He even got jealous of my gentleman friend, and then life became impossible. . . . 'Never mind, we'll go away and I'll have you all to myself,' he kept saying. But I knew that he only earned two thousand francs a month and had to give part of that to his mother.

"Well, he did what he'd said he'd do. . . . One evening he turned up, looking white as a sheet. . . . I was with my gentleman friend. . . . He sent the ground-floor tenant up to fetch me. . . .

" 'Mademoiselle Julie,' she told me, 'will you come down for a moment?' She'd realized, from the way he looked, that it was something serious. . . . He was standing there in the hall. . . . I can still picture him, beside the coatrack, under the colored light of the hall lamp.

" 'Is *he* there?' he growled between his teeth.

" 'What's the matter with you? Have you gone crazy?'

" 'You've got to come at once. . . . We're going to bolt.'

" 'What?'

" 'Bring whatever you can. . . . We're taking the midnight train. . . .' And then he whispered—and his breath smelled of liquor: 'I've taken the cashbox!'

"That was how it happened. What could I do? I told him to wait for me on the sidewalk. I went upstairs and told my friend that I'd just heard that my sister was having a baby and wanted me to come right away. . . .

"He suspected nothing, poor man. . . . He just looked disappointed, because of course, he hadn't had anything yet that evening. . . .

" 'Well, I'll try to come tomorrow.'

" 'That's right. You come tomorrow.'

"He went off. I lifted the blind and saw Jean waiting for me under the gas lamp at the corner of the street. . . . I stuffed some things into my suitcase . . . I had only one. . . . I had to leave some perfectly good dresses behind, and three pairs of shoes. . . . We took the night train. . . . He was very frightened. . . . He saw policemen everywhere. . . . When we got to Paris he didn't feel safe there, he wouldn't even stay at a hotel, for fear of being asked for his identity card, and we took the next train to Marseilles. . . .

"What could I have said to him? What's done is done. . . .

"We got here at night. . . . We wandered about the streets with our luggage for at least an hour before he could bring himself to go into a hotel."

She was devouring her andouillette, smeared with mustard, and from time to time nibbling a sour gherkin.

"He fell sick right away. . . . I looked after him. At night he had nightmares and kept talking to himself, trying to get up; I had to hold him down, he struggled so. . . .

"It went on for a whole week. And d'you know how much he'd taken? Twenty-five thousand francs . . . With that, he was going to take a boat to South America . . . only there weren't any in the port; all the ones on the list were sailing from Bordeaux. . . .

"Last night I felt stifled. I'd had enough of it, I needed air, and I told him I was going out for an hour. . . . I ought to have guessed that, jealous as he was, he'd follow me. . . . I may even have guessed it. . . . But I couldn't help myself. . . . Once outside I didn't even turn back. Two streets beyond this—I don't know the names of the streets—I saw a light like that of the Boule Rouge and I heard some music. . . . I had such a longing to dance that nothing could have stopped me. I went in. . . ."

She turned around sharply, as though at that very moment she had felt behind her the presence of the man she was thinking about, but it was only a young couple, so spruce and smiling that one could tell, at a glance, that they were on their honeymoon.

"I wonder where he can have gone. I know him, he's quite capable of having given himself up to the police. . . . Otherwise, if he's still prowling around Marseilles, he's quite capable of playing some dirty trick on me.

"I went dancing. . . . A real gentleman, who was in the orange trade, offered to see me home. . . . Just as I was leaving the dance hall with him I saw Jean standing on the edge of the sidewalk. . . .

"He didn't say a word to me. He started walking. I dropped the other fellow, whom I'd hardly recognize if I saw him again, and I rushed after him, calling 'Jean! Listen to me!'

"He went back to the hotel; his teeth were clenched and he was as white as this napkin. He began to pack his suitcase. He called me all sorts of names. . . .

"And yet I give you my word I loved him. . . . I even believe that if I were to see him again now . . ."

The crowds were thinning out around the tables. Cigarette smoke began to fill the room, with the smell of spirits and liqueurs.

"Coffee, *messieurs-dames?*"

There was another scene that had often struck Monsieur Monde, a scene one can glimpse in the streets of Paris when one peers into a restaurant through the window: facing one another across a table from which the meal has been cleared, with a soiled tablecloth, coffee cups, glasses of brandy or liqueur, a middle-aged stoutish man with a florid complexion and a happy though somewhat anxious look in his eyes, and a young woman holding her handbag up to her face and repainting the bow of her lips with the help of the mirror.

He had dreamed of that. He had envied them. Julie touched up her face, hunted in her handbag, called the waiter. "Have you got cigarettes?"

And presently her lips stained the pallid tip of a cigarette with a vivid pink that was more sensuously feminine than a woman's blood.

She had said everything. She had finished. Drained now, she stared at herself in the mirror over her companion's shoulder, and little furrows in her forehead betrayed the return of her anxiety.

It was not a question of love, now, but of survival. What exactly was she thinking? Two or three times she scrutinized the man with swift little glances, sizing him up, gauging his possible usefulness.

And he, ill at ease and aware of the stupidity of his question, stammered out: "What are you going to do?"

A curt shrug of the shoulders.

He had felt so envious of those who take no heed for the morrow and know none of the responsibilities with which other men burden themselves!

"Have you any money?"

Her eyes half closed because of the smoke she was exhaling; she picked up her bag and held it out to him.

He had already opened it the night before. He found it just as it was, with the cosmetics, a scrap of pencil, and a few crumpled notes, including a thousand-franc one.

She looked him sternly in the eyes, and then her lips formed a contemptuous, terribly contemptuous smile, as she said: "That's not what's worrying me, for sure!"

It was late. They were almost alone, now, in the deserted dining room, where the waiters were beginning to tidy up, and in one corner waitresses were already laying out cutlery for the evening meal.

"Waiter!"

"Coming, monsieur . . ."

And the fluttering figures were snapped up by the purple pencil and lined up on a pad of paper, one sheet of which was pulled off and laid on the cloth in front of Monsieur Monde.

He had a great deal of money in his wallet. He had slipped in as many notes as it would hold, and it embarrassed him to open it; he did so with reluctance, in the furtive manner of a miser; he realized that Julie had noticed, that she had seen the bundle and was once more observing him with a suspicious eye.

They rose at the same time, visited the cloakrooms, and then met again outside, in the sunshine, not knowing what to do, not knowing how to stay together or how to part company.

They walked automatically to the quayside and mingled with the people watching small boys or old men angling.

In another hour Madame Monde would step out of

her car before the police station on Rue La Roche-foucauld. He was not thinking of Madame Monde; he was not thinking of anything. He was conscious of moving restlessly in the midst of an outsize universe. His skin smelled springlike, because of the sunshine. His shoes were covered with fine dust. He was intensely aware of his companion's scent.

They had gone two hundred yards or so and were wandering aimlessly when she stopped.

"I don't feel like walking," she decided.

Then they retraced their steps, past the three-story restaurant with its wide windows where, now, only the bustling black-and-white figures of waiters could be seen. It seemed quite natural to walk up La Canebière, and in front of a brasserie whose striped awning was down, despite the time of year, Monsieur Monde suggested: "Would you like to sit down?"

And then they were sitting beside the window, on either side of a small marble-top table; in front of him there was a glass of beer on a cardboard mat, and in front of her a cup of coffee which she was not drinking.

She was waiting. She said: "I'm stopping you from going about your business."

"I have no business."

"That's true. You told me you had private means. Where d'you live?"

"I did live in Paris, but I've left."

"Without your wife?"

"Yes."

"On account of a chick?"

"No!"

Her eyes revealed bewilderment and, once again, suspicion.

"Why?"

"I don't know. . . . For no reason."

"Haven't you any children?"

"Yes . . ."

"And you didn't mind leaving them?"

"They're grown up. . . . My daughter's married. . . ."

Not far from them, people were playing bridge, important citizens and aware of their own importance, and two youths of Alain's age were playing billiards and looking at themselves in the glass.

"I don't want to sleep in that hotel again."

He realized that she wanted to avoid unpleasant memories. He made no reply. And a long silence fell. They sat there, still and heavy, in the gathering darkness. Soon the lights would go on. The window, close beside them, shed a kind of frozen halo on their cheeks.

Julie was scanning the crowd that streamed by along the sidewalk, perhaps because she had nothing else to do, or to keep herself in countenance, or else perhaps in hope—or in fear—of recognizing Jean.

"I don't think I'll stay in Marseilles," she said.

"Where will you go?"

"I don't know. . . . Farther on . . . Maybe to Nice? . . . Maybe to some small place by the sea where there won't be anybody. I'm sick of men. . . ."

At any moment they were free to get up and say good-by to one another, to go their different ways and never meet again. It seemed almost as if they did not know how to set about it, and that was why they stayed there.

Monsieur Monde felt embarrassed at sitting so long over a single drink, and summoned the waiter to order another half-pint. She called him back to ask: "When is there a train to Nice?"

"I'll bring you the timetable."

She handed it to Monsieur Monde, who looked up two trains, a fast one that left Marseilles at seven and another, at nine, that stopped all along the coast.

"Don't you find it gloomy here?"

The quietness was oppressive, the room seemed empty, there was too much unstirring air between the few customers, and every sound was detached, assumed importance: the exclamation of a card player, the click of billiard balls, the snap of the lid of the soiled-linen hamper as the waiter opened and closed it. The lights were switched on, but then, in the dusk, the slate-gray street proved a depressing sight, with its curious procession of men, women, and children, walking fast or slowly, brushing up against or pushing past one another, all strangers to the rest, each going God knows where and perhaps nowhere, while obese buses bore past their full loads of tight-packed humanity.

"Excuse me." The waiter, behind them, drew a

heavy red curtain along its brass rod, and with a single gesture abolished the outside world.

Monsieur Monde sighed, gazing at his glass of beer. He noticed that his companion's fingers were clenched on her handbag. And he seemed to have to make a long journey through time and space to find the simple, commonplace words that he uttered at last, which blended with the banality of the setting:

"Shall we take the nine o'clock train?"

She said nothing, but sat still; the fingers clutching the crocodile-skin bag relaxed. She lit a fresh cigarette, and it was later on, about seven o'clock, when the brasseries were full of customers drinking their apéritifs, that they went out, as grave and glum as a real married couple.

# Five

From time to time he frowned. The stare of his pale eyes became more intense. These were the only visible signs of his anguish, and yet at such moments he felt out of his depth, and if he had not retained a certain self-respect he would have been capable of tapping the shiny walls of the compartment to make sure they really existed.

He was in a train once more, a train that had the special smell of all night trains. Four of the compartments in the second-class carriage were dark, with drawn curtains, and when, a short while previously, looking for seats, he had opened doors at random, he had disturbed people who were sleeping.

He stood in the corridor, leaning against the wall which bore a number on an enamel plate. He had drawn up the blind in front of him, and the window was dark, cold, and clammy; occasional lights could be seen in little stations along the coast; by chance, his carriage invariably stopped in front of the lamps marked "Gentlemen" and "Ladies."

He was smoking a cigarette. He was conscious of smoking it, of holding it between his fingers, of blowing out the smoke, and this was what was so baffling, so bewildering; he was conscious of everything, he kept on seeing himself without the intermediary of a mirror, he would catch sight of one of his own gestures or attitudes and feel almost certain that he recognized it.

But he searched his memory in vain, he could not picture himself in any similar situation. Especially, without his mustache, and wearing a ready-made suit that somebody else had worn!

Even that instinctive movement . . . half turning his head to glance at Julie, in the corner of the compartment, sometimes sitting with eyes closed as though asleep, and sometimes staring straight in front of her as though wrestling with some important problem.

But Julie herself formed part of his memories. He felt no surprise at seeing her there. He recognized her. Perplexed, he resisted the notion of some previous existence.

And yet, often, he was sure of it—he had always intended to note it down in the morning, but had never done so—three or four times at least he had dreamed the same dream, he had found himself repeatedly in a flat-bottomed boat with oars that were too long and too heavy to handle, in a landscape whose details he could recall even when awake and long after, a landscape he had never seen in real life, made up of greenish lagoons and hills of that purplish blue that one sees in the paintings of early Italian masters.

Each time he had had that particular dream he had recognized the place, he had experienced the satisfaction that one feels on returning to a familiar spot.

But this was clearly impossible in the case of this train journey with Julie. He was clearheaded, rational.

This must be a scene that he had so often seen performed by other people, a scene that he had probably longed so violently to enact himself, that now . . .

That glance back into the compartment, that air of satisfaction that must have come over his face when he looked at his sleeping companion . . . And the woman's questioning gesture, that tilt of her chin when the train drew up noisily in a more important station and was invaded by a rush of new travelers; it meant: Where are we?

As the glazed door was closed, he mouthed the name so that she could read it on his lips, separating the syllables: "Toulon!" He repeated: "Tou-lon . . . Toulon . . ."

Failing to understand, she beckoned him to come in, showed him the vacant seat beside her, and he went and sat in it; his own voice had an unfamiliar ring.

"Toulon . . ."

She took a cigarette out of her bag. "Give me a light. . . ."

She called him "*tu*" for the first time, naturally, because for her, too, this was probably a moment that she had lived through before.

"Thanks . . . I think we'd better go on to Nice. . . ."

She was whispering. In the opposite corner an elderly man with white hair was asleep, and his wife, who was elderly too, was watching over him like a child. He must have been ill, for once before she had made him swallow a small greenish pill. She was watching Julie and Monsieur Monde. And he felt ashamed, because he guessed what she must be thinking about them. Moreover, although she dared not mention it, she probably resented Julie's smoking, which must upset the old man.

The train started off again.

"D'you know Nice?"

This time the "*tu*" came less naturally. Julie had had time to premeditate it. He felt convinced she was using it for the benefit of the lady opposite, and because it seemed more logical, conforming to a familiar situation.

"A little . . . Not very well . . ."

He had been there several times, three winters running in fact, with his first wife after the birth of their daughter, who as a baby had suffered from bronchitis every year; in those days doctors still recommended the Riviera. They had stayed in a big middle-class hotel on the Promenade des Anglais.

"I don't know it myself. . . ."

They fell silent. She finished her cigarette, which she had difficulty in crushing in the narrow brass ash tray, then she crossed and uncrossed her legs, which gleamed palely in the bluish shadows; she tried out various positions, sank back against the padded upholstery, and finally rested her head on her companion's shoulder.

This, too, was a memory that . . . No, surely! It was an attitude in which he'd seen other people a dozen times, a hundred times. He had tried to imagine their feelings and now he was acting in the scene himself, it

was he whom the young man standing in the corridor—
he must have got on at Toulon—was watching, with his
face glued to the window.

Then came the procession along the station platform, over the tracks, the slow monotonous scuffle
toward the exit, the search through his pockets for the
tickets. . . .

"I tell you you put them in the left-hand pocket of
your waistcoat. . . ."

She had reverted to "*vous.*" All around them, touts
were calling out the names of hotels, but she did not
listen to them. It was she who led the way. She walked
straight ahead, threading her way much more swiftly
than he could, and once they were through the gateway
she remarked: "We'd better leave our things in the
baggage room."

They had only one suitcase each, but Julie's was
heavy and particularly cumbersome.

Thus, once outside the station, they no longer
looked like travelers. They made straight for the town
center; it was a fine clear night, and there were still
some cafés open. From afar they could see the lights of
the Casino de la Jetée and their manifold reflections in
the water of the bay.

Julie showed neither surprise nor admiration.
Because she occasionally turned one of her high heels,
she clung to the man's arm, but it was she who led the
way. She went forward without speaking a word, as
calmly as an ant guided by its instinct.

"So this is the famous Promenade des Anglais?"

Branched lamps, stretching out to infinity. The vast sweep of the Promenade, all along the sea, with its small yellow paving stones and its deserted benches, and long lines of cars in front of casinos and grand hotels.

She was not dazzled by it all. She kept on walking, glanced down all the side streets, and finally turned down one of them and went close to the window of a brasserie to peer through the gap between the curtains.

"We might try this one."

"It's a café," he objected.

But she pointed out beyond the café and in the same building, a door with the word "Hotel" in white letters. They went into the brightly lit room, and she collapsed, somewhat wearily, onto a crimson seat; her next gesture, since there were people about, was to open her handbag, hold her mirror up to her face, and redden her lips.

"Will you have supper?" the waiter asked.

She said to Monsieur Monde: "D'you want to eat?"

They had not had dinner at Marseilles, because although they might have done so before the train left, they had not felt hungry then.

"What have you got?"

"Some excellent ravioli . . . onion soup to start with if you like . . . or a rare steak . . ."

Several tables were occupied by people having supper, and the waiter set their places in front of them. In spite of the bright electric lights, a certain gray weariness pervaded the air. The people present were speaking little and eating conscientiously, as at a regular meal.

"In the left-hand corner, look," she whispered to him.

"Who is it?"

"Don't you recognize him? . . . It's Parsons, one of the three Parsons brothers, the flying-trapeze acrobats. . . . That's his wife with him. She ought never to wear a suit, it makes her look like a teapot. . . . She's in their act now, in place of Lucien, the brother who had an accident in Amsterdam. . . ."

They were very ordinary-looking people; the man, who was about thirty-five, might have been a well-dressed workman.

"They must be in a show here. . . . Oh, look! Three tables away . . ."

She brightened up, all her apathy had vanished, and to emphasize her remarks she kept laying her hand on her companion's wrist so as to compel his admiration.

"Jeanine Dor! The singer!"

This was a woman whose raven-black, oily hair hung down on either side of her cheeks; she had enormous, deeply ringed eyes in a pallid face, and her mouth was a crimson gash. Alone at a table, with a tragic disdainful air, her coat flung back behind her, she was eating spaghetti.

"She must be over fifty. . . . But she's still the only person who can hold an audience breathless for over an hour, just with her songs. . . . I'll have to ask her for her autograph."

She rose suddenly and went up to the proprietor, who was standing by the cashier's desk. Monsieur Monde had no idea what she was going to do. Their food was brought, and he waited. He could see her talking self-confidently, then the proprietor turned to glance at him with apparent approval, and she returned.

"Give me the baggage-room ticket."

She took it off, and then came back.

"They've got a room with two beds. . . .You don't mind, do you? For one thing, they probably wouldn't have had two single rooms vacant. . . . And then it wouldn't have looked natural! . . . Oh, look! Those four girls to the right of the door . . . They're dancers. . . ."

She was eating with the same concentration as at Marseilles, but without missing anything that was going on around them.

"The proprietor tells me it's still early. The music halls have closed but they won't start coming in from casinos and night clubs till after three. . . . I wonder . . ."

He did not understand at first. The girl wore an obstinate frown. She must be contemplating a job.

"The food's good here, and not too dear. I gather the rooms are clean."

They were drinking their coffee when a boy came to

tell them their luggage had come and been taken up into the bedroom. Julie, despite the previous night's ordeal, did not seem to be sleepy. She was watching Jeanine Dor going out, through a side door, to the hotel staircase.

"They all stay here. In an hour there'll be some more of them. . . ."

But an hour was too long and dreary a wait. She smoked one more cigarette, and then rose with a yawn.

It was not until the third day that they made love. A confused three days. Their room, which overlooked a narrow courtyard, was furnished only with drab old things, a grayish threadbare carpet on the floor, a tapestry-covered armchair, wallpaper that was more brown than yellow, and in one corner a screen hiding the washbasin and bidet.

The first night Julie had undressed behind the screen, emerging in blue-striped pajamas. But finding the trousers uncomfortable, she had discarded them during the night.

He slept badly, in the next bed, separated from hers by a bedside table and a narrow mat. His supper was giving him indigestion. Several times, hearing sounds from the brasserie below, he had been tempted to go downstairs to ask for bicarbonate of soda.

He got up at eight, dressed noiselessly, without awakening his companion, who had flung back her bedclothes, for the radiator was boiling hot, the room overheated and airless. Perhaps that was why he had felt so uncomfortable during the night.

He went downstairs, leaving his suitcase clearly visible lest Julie think he had gone for good. The coffee room was empty. There was nobody to serve him and he went to have breakfast in a bar full of workmen and clerks, then walked along the seashore without thinking of that other sea by the edge of which he had dreamed of lying weeping.

Perhaps he needed to get used to things? The sky was a very pale, babyish blue, the sea too, like the sea in a schoolchild's watercolor, the gulls were chasing one another, white in the sunshine, and water carts were tracing wet patterns on the paving.

When he got back, at about eleven, he felt compelled to knock at the door.

"Come in. . . ."

She could not have known it was he. She was wearing only her panties and her brassière. She had plugged an electric iron into the socket of the lamp and was pressing her black silk dress.

She asked him: "Did you sleep all right?"

Her breakfast tray was on the bedside table.

"I'll be ready in half an hour. . . . What time is it? Eleven? Would you wait for me downstairs?

He waited, reading a local paper. He was growing used to waiting. They lunched alone together again. Then they went out, and they had scarcely reached the Promenade des Anglais, up near the Casino de la Jetée, when she asked him to wait yet again and disappeared into the Casino.

Next she dragged him down a street in the town center. "Wait for me. . . ."

On an enamel plate there was a Greek name, followed by the word "Impresario."

She came back in a fury.

"He's a pig!" she announced, without further explanation. "If you'd rather go off and walk by yourself . . ."

"Where are you going?"

"I've got two more addresses. . . ."

Grim and tight-lipped, she strode along the unfamiliar city streets, questioned policemen, climbed flights of stairs, and kept pulling scraps of paper with new addresses out of her bag.

"I know the place we must go to for an apéritif. . . ."

This was the Cintra, the fashionable bar. She renewed her make-up before going in. She put on a jaunty air. He understood that she was wishing he were better dressed. She was even wondering whether he would know how to behave in a place like this, and it was she who gave the order with an air of authority, as she climbed onto a high stool and crossed her legs:

"Two pink gins, barman . . ."

She nibbled some olives, ostentatiously. She stared boldly at men and women. It infuriated her to know nobody, to be merely a newcomer rating only a supercilious glance because of her cheap little dress and her shabby coat.

"Let's go and have dinner. . . ."

She knew where to go for dinner too. Afterward, with a certain embarrassment, she began: "Would you mind going back by yourself? . . . Oh, it's not what you might think. . . . After what I've been through, I can tell you I've had enough of men and you won't catch me at that again. But I don't want to be a burden on you. You've got your own life to lead, haven't you? You've been very kind. . . . I'm sure that backstage I shall meet people I know. . . . At Lille I used to meet all the artistes on tour. . . ."

He did not go to bed, but walked about the streets alone. Then, at one point, because he was tired of walking, he went into a movie house. And this was another familiar image, drawn from the remote mysterious depths of his memory: an aging man, all by himself, being guided by an attendant with a flashlight into a darkened room where a film has already begun, where voices boom and men larger than life gesticulate on the screen.

When he got back to Gerly's—that was the name of his hotel and of the brasserie—he caught sight of Julie sitting at a table in the café with the group of acrobats. She saw him go past. He realized that she was talking about him. He went upstairs, and she came to join him a quarter of an hour later, and this time she undressed in front of him.

"He's promised to put in a word for me. . . . He's a decent sort. His father, who was Italian, was a bricklayer by trade, and he himself started off in the same way. . . ."

Another day passed, and then another, and Monsieur Monde was getting used to things; he had even stopped thinking about them. After lunch, that third day, Julie decided: "I'm going to have an hour's sleep. . . . I got back late last night. . . . Aren't you going to have a nap?"

He felt sleepy too, as a matter of fact. They went up one behind the other, and meanwhile he had a vision of other couples, hundreds of couples, going up flights of stairs in the same way. And a slight flush rose to his cheeks.

The room had not been done. The two beds, unmade, revealed the livid whiteness of sheets, and there were traces of lipstick on Julie's pillow.

"Aren't you going to undress?"

Usually, when he took a siesta—and in Paris, in the course of his former life, he had done so from time to time—he would lie down fully dressed, with a newspaper spread out under his feet. He took off his jacket, then his waistcoat. Julie, with that snakelike movement which he was beginning to recognize, drew her dress up along her body and slipped it over her head.

She showed no surprise when he came up to her, with a rather shamefaced look. She was obviously expecting it.

"Draw the curtains."

And she lay down, making room for him beside her. She was thinking about something else. Every time he looked at her he saw that now familiar frown on her forehead.

On the whole, she was not sorry about it; things seemed more natural this way. But fresh problems occurred to her, and suddenly she lost all desire for sleep. Her head propped on her hand, her elbow on the pillow, she gazed at him with fresh interest as if from now on she had acquired the right to call him to account.

"What do you actually do?"

And as he failed to grasp the exact meaning of the question, she went on:

"You told me, the first day, that you had private means. People in your position don't go gallivanting about all by themselves. Or else surely they live in a different style. . . . What did you do before?"

"Before what?"

"Before you went off?"

Thus she was making her way toward the truth as unfailingly as, landing in Nice in the middle of the night, she had made her way toward this hotel, where she was at home.

"You've got a wife. . . . You told me you had children. . . . How did you go off?"

"I just went!"

"Did you have a row with your wife?"

"No."

"Is she young?"

"About my age."

"I understand. . . ."

"What d'you understand?"

"You just wanted to have a good time! . . . And

when you've spent all your money, or when you're tired . . ."

"No . . . It's not that."

"What happened, then?"

And he replied, with a sense of shame, chiefly because he felt he was spoiling everything by such stupid words, blurted out on that tumbled bed, in front of those bared breasts that no longer tempted him: "I'd had enough of it."

"Have it your own way!" she sighed.

She took this opportunity to slip behind the screen to wash, which she had been too lazy to do immediately after making love; from here she went on:

"You're a funny sort of fellow!"

He put on his clothes again. He no longer felt sleepy. He was not unhappy. This squalid drabness was all part of what he had been seeking.

"Would you like to stay on at Nice?" she asked, emerging naked with a towel in her hand.

"I don't know. . . ."

"You're not fed up with me too? . . . You know, you must tell me honestly. I keep wondering how we happen to have got hitched together. . . . It's not really like me. Parsons has promised to look after me. . . . He's in well with the man who runs the floor shows at the 'Pingouin.' . . . I shan't be out of a job for long. . . ."

Why was she talking of leaving him? He did not want that. He tried to tell her so.

"It suits me all right like this. . . ."

She looked at him, as he tried to pull his braces over his shoulders, and she burst out laughing, the first time he had heard her laugh.

"You're a scream! Well . . . When you feel like clearing off, you just say so. . . . If I may give you one piece of advice, it's to buy yourself another outfit. . . . You're not miserly, by any chance?"

"No . . ."

"Then you'd do better to dress decently. If you like, I'll go with you. Didn't your wife have any taste at all?"

She was lying down again, lighting a cigarette and sending the smoke up to the ceiling.

"Above all, if it's a question of money, don't be afraid to tell me. . . ."

"I've got money. . . ."

The bundle of notes, wrapped up in newspaper, was still in the suitcase, and he glanced at this instinctively. Since coming to Gerly's he had given up locking it, for fear of offending his companion. Under pretext of looking for something in it, he made sure the bundle was still there.

"Are you going out? Will you come back and get me about five o'clock?"

That afternoon he spent sitting on a bench on the Promenade, his head bent, his eyes half closed in the sunshine, with the blue of the sea before him and the occasional flash of gulls' wings as they crossed his horizon.

He never stirred. Children played around him, and sometimes a hoop came to rest between his legs, or a ball was thrown toward him. He seemed to be asleep. His face looked thicker and flabbier and his lips hung half open. Several times he gave a start, thinking he heard the voice of Monsieur Lorisse, his cashier. Not for one moment did he think of his wife or children, but it was the meticulous old clerk who appeared in his dream.

He remained heedless of time, and it was Julie who eventually came to look for him and remarked: "I was sure I'd find you flopping on a bench."

Why? This question bothered him for some little while.

"Let's go and buy you some clothes before the shops shut. . . . You see, I think of you and not of myself. . . ."

"I must go and get some money from the hotel. . . ."

"D'you leave your money in the bedroom? That's a mistake. Especially if there's a lot of it. . . ."

She waited for him below. He took a bundle of ten thousand francs, so as not to unfasten the pin. The maid was cleaning the hallway, but she could not see him, for he had closed the door. Julie's words had made him anxious. He climbed onto a chair and pushed the parcel on top of the wardrobe.

She took him to an English firm where they sold smart ready-made clothes. She chose his outfit for him: gray flannel trousers and a navy blue double-breasted jacket.

"With a cap, you'd pass for a yachtsman!"

She insisted on his buying summer shoes of brown and white leather.

"You look quite different. . . . I sometimes wonder . . ."

She said no more, but merely cast a furtive glance at him.

She must already have been to the Cintra on her own, for when they went in the barman made some imperceptible sign to her and a young man winked at her.

"You don't look exactly cheerful. . . ."

They drank. They ate. They went to the Casino, where Julie stayed for a couple of hours and after winning two or three thousand francs ended by losing all that was left in her purse.

Vexed, she motioned to him: "Let's go back."

They had already formed the habit of walking side by side; when she was tired she clung to his arm. They slowed down automatically a few yards before their hotel, like people who are going home.

She did not want to go through the brasserie.

They closed their door. She bolted it, for it was always she who took this precaution.

"Where d'you hide your money?"

He pointed to the wardrobe.

"I'd take care if I were you. . . ."

He climbed onto the same chair as that afternoon, passed his hand across the top of the wardrobe, but felt nothing but a thick layer of dust.

"Well, what's up?"

He stood there, aghast. She grew impatient.

"Have you turned into a statue?"

"The parcel's gone."

"The money?"

Suspicious by nature, she refused to believe him.

"Let's see. . . ."

She was not tall enough, even when she stood on the chair. She cleared the table and climbed up on that.

"How much was there?"

"About three hundred thousand francs, or a little less . . ."

"What did you say?"

He felt ashamed, now, of the vastness of the sum. "Three hundred thousand . . ."

"We must tell the proprietor at once and send for the police. Wait. . . ."

He held her back. "No. It's not possible."

"Why not? Are you crazy?"

"We mustn't. I'll explain why. . . . And in any case it doesn't matter, I'll manage somehow. . . . I'll send for some more money. . . ."

"Are you as rich as all that?"

She seemed resentful now, as though she were annoyed with him for having deceived her, and she lay down without a word, turning her back on him, and answered his good night with a mere grunt.

# Six

It was bitter and yet sweet, like the sort of pain that one cherishes and tends solicitously for fear of seeing it disappear. Monsieur Monde felt no anger, no resentment, no regret. About his fourteenth or fifteenth year, while he was at the Lycée, he had gone through a period of acute mysticism following a Lenten fast. He had devoted his days and part of his nights to spiritual exercises in search of perfection, and he had happened to keep a photograph of himself at that time—in a group, for he would have scorned to have his own likeness taken. He looked thinner and rather mournful, with a smile whose sweetness infuriated him later, when the reaction had set in.

Another time, much later, after his second marriage, his wife had given him to understand that she found a smoker's breath offensive. He had given up not only tobacco but any sort of spirits and even wine. He derived a savage satisfaction from this mortification of the flesh. This time again he had lost weight, so much so that after three weeks he'd had to go to the tailor's to have his suits altered.

It mattered little, now, whether they fitted him well or badly; but in the last two months he had lost weight far more drastically. He felt all the livelier for it. And although his once rosy complexion was now sallow, he would look with some complacency, when the occasion arose, at the reflection of a face that spoke not only of serenity but of a secret joy, an almost morbid delectation.

The hardest struggle was to keep awake. He had always been a big eater. Now, for instance, at four in the morning, he had to resort to various devices to stop himself from falling asleep.

This was the moment, moreover, when general weariness pervaded the Monico like drifting dust. For the second time Monsieur René, who called himself Artistic Director, had come into the pantry, impeccably dressed in dinner jacket and immaculate white waistcoat, with his teeth gleaming aggressively.

Monsieur Monde could watch him coming through the room, for close to him at eye level there was a minute round spy-hole that enabled him to keep watch, not so much on the guests as on the staff.

Monsieur René could not help smiling to right and left as he walked, like a prince distributing favors. He moved along in this fashion in the glowing light of the dance hall, reached the folding doors, which were hung with red velvet on one side but shabby and squalid on the other, and at the precise moment when he pushed them open with a practiced hand his smile disappeared, and there was no more sign of his splendid teeth; he was a quadroon from Martinique, whose hair was almost sleek, but whose bluish nails betrayed his mixed blood.

"What's the time, Désiré?"

For the time is never publicly displayed in a place where so much art is used to make people forget time.

Désiré was Monsieur Monde, who had chosen the name himself. Désiré Clouet. It had first occurred to him at Marseilles, when he was sitting with Julie in a brasserie on La Canebière and the girl had asked his name. Caught off his guard, he had been incapable of inventing one. Across the street, over a cobbler's shop, he had read a name in yellow letters: "Désiré Clouet, shoemaker."

Now he was Désiré to some people, and Monsieur Désiré to the rank and file of the staff. The pantry was a long, narrow room that had once been the kitchen of a private house. The green-painted walls were turning yellowish and, here and there, the color of tobacco juice. A door at the far end gave onto the back stairs. As this made it possible to leave the place by a street different from that in which the main entrance was situated, guests occasionally came through Monsieur Désiré's domain.

These were mainly the clients of the gaming tables, who were not offended by dirt and disorder. They did not mind seeing that the kitchens of the Monico consisted of a wretched gas stove whose red rubber tubing was forever coming apart, and which was merely used for warming up dishes brought in from a nearby bistro. There was no sink. Greasy plates and cutlery were stacked in baskets. Only the glasses, marked with the letter M, were washed on the spot and put away in a cupboard. On the floor, under the table, bottles of champagne were waiting, and on that same table open tins of foie gras, ham, pieces of cold meat were laid out.

Désiré's place was in the corner, against the wall of the dance hall, on a kind of platform where there was a desk. He replied: "Four o'clock, Monsieur René."

"Soon be through now!"

Apart from the hostesses, there were scarcely half a dozen guests in the hall, and they had stopped dancing; the band took long rests between their numbers and Monsieur René was obliged to call them to order from afar, with a barely perceptible movement of his hands.

Monsieur René was eating. Almost every time he came into the pantry he ate something, a truffle that he'd pull out of the foie gras with his fingers, a piece of ham, a spoonful of caviar, or he would drain a bottle; if he felt like a square meal he would make himself a substantial sandwich and eat it slowly, his cuffs turned back, perched on a corner of the table, which he had carefully wiped.

There were long intervals, like this, when Désiré had nothing to do. He had been given the title of steward. He was in charge of everything in the pantry: food and drink, cigarettes, accessories for the *cotillon*; he had to see that nothing left the room without being entered on a slip of paper, and then make sure through his spy-hole that the customer received that particular slip and no other, for waiters are up to all sorts of tricks; one night they'd had to strip one of them to find the money he denied having taken.

Julie was there in the orange-lighted dance hall. Her

customers had all gone. She was sitting at a table with Charlotte, a plump blonde; they were exchanging idle remarks, pretending to drink, and getting up to dance together every time Monsieur René came past and snapped his fingers.

It was Julie who had introduced Monsieur Désiré to the Monico. The first evening, on discovering that his money had vanished, he had wanted to go away. Anywhere, he didn't care where. It was she who had been indignant to see him accept the situation so naturally, for she was incapable of understanding how such an event could come almost as a relief.

And yet this was so. It was bound to happen. He had made a mistake, in Paris, through maladroitness or through timidity perhaps, when he provided himself with so large a sum of money. In so doing he had not followed the rule, a rule that was unwritten but which existed nonetheless. When he had decided to go off he had felt no surprise or emotion, because he knew it had to happen. By contrast, when he had gone to the bank to withdraw the three hundred thousand francs he had felt embarrassed and guilty.

On those other two occasions when he had dreamed of escaping, had he thought about money? No. He had to be quite destitute, out in the street.

And now this had happened at last.

"Wait a minute. I've got something to say to the proprietor."

Julie had gone downstairs. When she came back a few minutes later she announced: "I was quite right.

. . . Where would you have gone? . . . There's a little room free, up at the top. . . . It's a servant's room, but Fred rents it by the month, quite cheap. I'll keep this room myself for a day or two and if I don't find anything I'll join you up on the sixth floor. . . . I'm sure I'll find something!"

She had found herself a job first, as hostess at the Monico, and then a few days later she had found him the position that he had now held for nearly two months.

They had practically nothing in common now. Occasionally, when Julie was on her own, they would go off to their hotel together in the small hours. She would tell him stories about René or about the boss, Monsieur Dodevin, stories about her fellow hostesses and her customers; he would listen patiently, nodding his head and smiling beatifically. So much so that she lost patience.

"What sort of man are you?"

"Why?"

"I don't know. . . . You're always contented. You don't mind how you're treated. . . . For one thing, you never brought a complaint, and yet you're not afraid of the police. . . . I noticed that, you may be sure! . . . You say good morning to that bitch that stole your money, when you meet her on the stairs. . . ."

Julie was convinced—and he felt inclined to agree with her—that it was the chambermaid on their floor, an ugly girl with greasy hair and big slack breasts, who had taken the bundle of notes from the top of the wardrobe; for she was just the type to spy on guests in their bedrooms, being always on the prowl in passages with a duster or a broom in her hand as an excuse.

Julie had discovered that she had as a lover a musician from the Casino who treated her with contempt.

"I bet you whatever you like that he's got the money now. He's too cunning to use it right away. He's waiting till the end of the season. . . ."

It was quite possible. And what of it?

This, again, was something he had dreamed of. Perhaps, indeed, it was just for this that he had left home? He often wondered about that. As a young man, when he passed a certain sort of woman in the darkness, particularly in sordid streets, he felt a great thrill of excitement. He would brush by them deliberately, but he never turned around; on the contrary, he would make his escape hurriedly as soon as they spoke a word to him.

Sometimes, especially in winter, he used to leave his office on Rue Montorgueil and spend a quarter of an hour wandering, through drizzling rain, in the mean streets around Les Halles, where certain lights seem redolent of mysterious debauchery.

Every time he had taken the train, alone or with his wife, every single time, he had felt a pang of envy, as he sat in his first-class carriage, of the people carrying shabby bundles and going off somewhere or other, careless of what awaited them elsewhere.

There was a night watchman on Rue Montorgueil, a former schoolmaster who had lost his job because of misconduct with his girl pupils. He was ill-dressed and unkempt. He would take up his post in the evening with a bottle of wine in his pocket and settle down in a small cubbyhole where he warmed up his supper over an alcohol burner.

On some mornings when Monsieur Monde arrived very early because of urgent business, he had surprised the man tidying things up, calm and unconcerned, on a last round to make sure that all was in order and then slipping off down the street in the bright early sunlight.

Where did he go? Nobody had ever discovered where he lived, in what corner he would go to ground, like an animal, during the daytime.

Monsieur Monde had actually envied him too.

And now Monsieur Désiré had begun to look like him.

"What d'you want, boy?"

The busboy had just rushed into the pantry; he had come, needless to say, to speak to Monsieur René, who was still busy eating.

"Is the boss up there?"

"Why?"

"There's a dick coming up, a dick I don't know who wants to speak to him."

Immediately, Monsieur René's thigh slid off the table, the sandwich vanished, he wiped his fingers, brushed his lapels, as swiftly as though with a single movement, and he sped across the dance floor, with enough self-control not to break into a run but to go on smiling at his guests.

Just as he reached the main door, which led onto the marble staircase, it opened to let in a man who had refused to leave his overcoat in the cloakroom, and whom Monsieur René greeted solicitously.

Désiré watched them through the little spy-hole. Julie and her friend, at their table, had grasped what was happening. Monsieur René could be seen inviting the detective to sit down at a table at some distance from the dance floor, but the policeman remained standing, shaking his head and speaking a few words; then Monsieur René disappeared through another door, the one that led to the gaming room. Other policemen, those who were on good terms with the establishment, had free access to this room, but it was wiser not to let a new man in.

He was a tall, strapping fellow of thirty-five. He waited, staring vaguely at the commonplace décor of the dance hall. Then Monsieur René reappeared, accompanied by the boss, Monsieur Dodevin, a former lawyer who had retained the outward dignity of his calling.

Once more the man was invited to sit down and have a bottle of champagne, but once more he refused. Then he was brought up to Désiré's den.

"Come in here," Monsieur Dodevin said. "We can talk better here. . . . René!"

"Yes, monsieur . . ." And René, who had understood, picked out a good bottle of champagne among those that were left, and polished two glasses from the cupboard.

"As you see, we haven't much room here. . . ."

And Monsieür Dodevin, who was invariably of a fine marble pallor, stepped into the dance hall for a moment to get two chairs covered in red velvet.

"Do sit down. . . . Are you from the Nice squad? . . . No? . . . I thought I hadn't met you before. . . ."

Désiré was not watching them. He was keeping his professional watch on the dance hall, where everyone was impatiently waiting for the departure of the last guests, who lingered stubbornly, thus preventing twenty people from going off to bed.

Julie, who knew he was up there although she could not see his face, kept signaling to him from a distance: "What's up? Something serious?"

He could not reply. It didn't matter. Julie felt the occasional need to make contact with him in this way, pulling a face for instance, when she was afflicted with a bad dancing partner or a ludicrous companion.

He heard a whispered mention of the Empress, and he listened keenly.

"Really? Is she dead?" murmured the ex-lawyer in an appropriately solemn tone. "Such an amazing woman . . . And you say she died shortly after leaving here? Of course it's sad, a great misfortune, but I don't see how . . ."

Only the night before, the Empress had been there,

barely five yards away from Désiré, who, though himself unseen, could examine her at leisure.

Who had first called her the Empress? It was hard to say. Probably she had borne that nickname for a long time on the Riviera. Some ten days earlier, Flip, the busboy, had rushed in, just as he had done when the policeman arrived, and had then announced to Monsieur René: "Good! Here comes the Empress!"

They had seen her come in, huge, obese, tallow-faced, a fur coat open on a bosom loaded with jewels. Under their puffy lids her eyes were so utterly lacking in expression that they seemed dead.

She was panting, from having climbed the stairs, for the Monico was on the first floor. She halted, like a queen waiting to be ceremoniously attended to. René hurried to welcome her, all smiles, bowing and scraping, pointing out one table and then another, finally leading her to a settee, while the Empress's companion, who carried a small Pekingese dog, followed with the modest bearing of a lady-in-waiting.

Désiré had not flinched that evening. Perhaps he had smiled a little more bitterly.

The Empress's companion was his first wife, Thérèse, whom he had not seen for eighteen years. Much as she had altered, he recognized her, and he felt no hatred, no resentment, only a sort of extra burden on his shoulders, added to the heavy weight they already bore, which he no longer even attempted to shake off.

Thérèse must be about forty now, scarcely more, for she had been eighteen when he married her. She looked older than her age. Her features had become set. She still looked rosy, but there must be a layer of cosmetics on her face to give it that disturbing, mask-like immobility.

When she smiled, however, and she happened to smile several times, it was almost the same smile he remembered, a timid, ingenuous, delightfully childish smile, the smile that for years had misled Monsieur Monde about his wife's nature.

She had been modest, self-effacing, apt to incline her head a little and say, in the gentlest voice: "Just as you please . . ."

Or else: "You know I like whatever you do. . . ."

A sudden movement would have shattered her, and yet she was the woman who had collected, in her desk, those obscene photographs that men thrust into strangers' hands on the Grands Boulevards; who had annotated them, copying them carefully, exaggerating the size of the sexual organs: she, again—her husband had found out almost for certain, although he had not wished to pursue his inquiry any further—who had sought out their chauffeur in his attic bedroom and who, when he drove her into town, had him stop in front of dubious apartment houses.

Afterward she resumed her pure smile as she bent over her children's cots.

Her eyelids were wrinkled now, but they had

retained a certain charm, reminding one of those flower petals which, as they shrivel, take on an ethereal transparency.

The detective now accepted the champagne he was being offered, the Havana cigar that Désiré hastily entered on the expense account, since this was his responsibility and eventually he would have to get the boss himself to sign a chit for it.

"They were both living in the Plaza," the policeman explained. "A magnificent apartment overlooking the Promenade . . . You can't imagine in what chaos and filth they lived. . . . They wouldn't let the hotel staff clean up for them. They had a maid, a Czech or something of the sort, who brought up their meals on a tray and served them, usually in bed, for they often lay in bed for thirty hours at a stretch. . . . When I got there with my colleague there were torn stockings in every corner, dirty linen all mixed up with jewelry and furs, money lying about on the furniture. . . ."

"What did she die of?" inquired Monsieur Dodevin.

And as Monsieur René was standing behind them, he motioned him to leave the room. The detective drew from his pocket a metal box, from which he took out a hypodermic syringe, dismantled, and showed it to Monsieur Dodevin, looking him in the eyes.

The ex-lawyer did not turn a hair, but merely shook his head, saying: "No, never that . . ."

"Indeed!"

"I give you my sacred word of honor that no morphine has ever come into this place, nor gone out of it. . . . You know my business as well as I do. . . . I don't claim to keep always strictly within the law, for that's impossible. Your colleagues on the Gambling Squad, who often come to see me in quite a friendly way, will tell you I'm above-board. I keep as close a watch on my staff as possible. I've engaged a man specially . . ." (he indicated Désiré) ". . . specially to make sure that nothing illegal goes on in the hall. . . . Tell me, Monsieur Désiré, have you ever seen any morphine here?"

"No, monsieur."

"Do you keep an eye on the waiters, the busboy, and the flower girls when they go up to the guests?"

"Yes, monsieur."

"You see, Inspector, if you'd mentioned cocaine I might not have been so categorical. I play fair. I don't try to pretend what isn't true. With the sort of women we're obliged to accept here, it's inevitable that one day or another we get one who's hooked on snow. That soon becomes obvious. I nearly always notice it after a few days. It happened a couple of months ago, and I got rid of her immediately. . . ."

The detective may have believed him, or he may not. He was staring impassively at his surroundings, and cast an apparently casual eye over Désiré.

The latter was somewhat alarmed. Six days exactly after he left Paris, the day after his money had been stolen, his photograph had appeared in the newspapers, not on the front page, like those of wanted criminals, but on the third, sandwiched unobtrusively between two advertisements. It was a bad likeness.

*"Handsome reward offered for information as to the above person, who is probably suffering from loss of memory."*

There followed the description of the clothes he had been wearing the day he disappeared and finally the address of a Paris lawyer, Madame Monde's own lawyer, who was looking after a lawsuit that she had been carrying on for ten years about property in which she was co-heir with some cousins.

Nobody had recognized him. He had not reflected for one moment that, if they were trying to find him, it was because the key of the safe was useless without his presence, or at any rate his signature.

"Was she wealthy?"

They were talking about the Empress.

"She had a fair amount left. . . . Only a few years ago she was worth tens of millions. . . . Actually she's an American, daughter of a garment manufacturer. She's been married four or five times. She's lived all over the place. She's been the wife of a Russian prince, among others, and that's why they call her the Empress. . . ."

"And the other woman?"

Désiré averted his eyes and looked into the dance hall, dreading the detective's watchful eye.

"A Frenchwoman, of a decent family. Divorced . . . She's done all sorts of things too. . . . When the Empress met her, she was a manicurist. . . ."

"Have you arrested her?"

"What's the use? . . . There were men involved too. . . . The hotel staff aren't communicative. They used to have people up to their bedrooms some evenings . . . nobody knows for sure, people they picked up goodness knows where, whom the staff were quite surprised to meet on the stairs of the hotel, and preferred not to see, you understand?"

The ex-lawyer understood perfectly.

"Yesterday morning, about ten o'clock, the Czech maid went down to ask for a doctor's phone number. When the doctor got there the Empress was dead already, and the other woman, still under the influence of the drug, seemed quite unaware of what had happened. . . . Your good health!"

"And yours!"

"I was obliged to come here. We're trying to find out where the morphine comes from. . . . This is the second case this winter. . . ."

"I told you . . ."

"Of course . . . of course . . ."

"Another cigar? Take a handful; they're not bad. . . ."

The detective did not demur; he slipped the cigars into the outside pocket of his jacket and picked up his hat.

"You can go out this way. . . ."

The door of the back staircase creaked. The boss

switched on the light and waited to turn it off till the policeman had reached the bottom of the stairs. Then he retraced his steps and put away the cigars in the box.

"Five, Désiré . . ."

"I've entered them, monsieur." And Désiré handed him a pencil with which to sign the form.

"That's how one gets involved in things!"

He went off to join Monsieur René in the dance hall. They stood near the door, arguing in low voices.

Julie was sitting with her legs crossed, swinging her left foot, to let Désiré know she was fed up. A waiter burst in and seized two empty champagne bottles from a basket under the table.

"I'm taking advantage of the least drunk of them having gone to the toilet!"

His customers were completely hoodwinked. Only the hostesses noticed the trick; the two bottles went to join those that the guests had drunk, and Désiré calmly put down two little crosses in his book.

He wondered what was going to become of his ex-wife. When she was a girl her parents had called her "Baby" because of her angelic look. The Empress was unlikely to have left her any money. Women of that sort never think of making a will.

He felt no resentment against her. Neither did he forgive her; it was unnecessary.

"Check for Number 9!" a headwaiter called out through the crack of the swinging door.

When the guests at Table 9 had gone it would be the end. They were paying. The cloakroom attendant was waiting behind them with their things. She was quite young and fresh-looking, dressed in shiny black, with a dark red ribbon in her hair. A doll. A plaything. She was engaged to a pork butcher's assistant, but Monsieur René made her sleep with him. Désiré suspected the boss of doing the same thing, but she was so secretive that one could never know the truth.

There was a scraping of chairs, noisy comings and goings, while the waiters, as they cleared the tables, drained the bottles and each ate something or other.

"A glass for me, Monsieur René!" Julie was thirsty, and he brought her one.

"It's been agony all evening! I was wearing my new shoes and I couldn't stand on my feet. . . ." She pulled off her little gold slippers and put on her street shoes, which were standing beside the gas stove.

Désiré was finishing his accounts, and the gamblers could now be heard crossing the dance hall on their way out. They were respectable citizens, all men, mostly tradespeople of Nice who, as such, were not allowed to visit the gambling rooms at the Casino. They shook hands as they parted, like fellow workers in an office.

"Are you coming, Désiré?"

Charlotte lived in the same hotel as they did. Day had dawned, and the town was deserted. Out at sea they could see white fishing boats with green-and-red-painted rims.

"Is it true that the Empress is dead?"

Désiré walked between the two of them. At one

street corner they stopped automatically in front of a
little bar that had just opened. A good smell rose from
the percolator, which the proprietor, in a blue apron,
was just polishing.

"Three coffees . . ."

They were blinking a little. They always had a peculiar aftertaste in their mouths. And the smell of the
night club still hung about the two women, who were
wearing their evening dresses under their street coats.
Theirs was a special sort of weariness, in their heads
rather than in their limbs.

They started off again. At Gerly's, the door was left
unlocked all night. The blinds of the brasserie were
still down.

They went upstairs slowly. Julie's room was on the
second floor and Charlotte's on the fourth. Désiré still
slept up in the attic.

They stopped on the landing to say good night to one
another. Julie, wholly unembarrassed by her friend's
presence, glanced up at him. "Coming?"

He did so occasionally; but now he said no. He didn't
feel like it. He went on upstairs.

"She's a nice girl," Charlotte said. "She's swell!"

He agreed.

"Good night . . ."

"Good night . . ."

He went on climbing, slowly. Once, at home on Rue
Ballu, he had climbed the stairs to his bedroom, an
evening when he had been out alone and his wife, the
second wife, was waiting for him. And without know-

ing, under a sort of compulsion, he had stopped and sat down on a step, wearily, without a thought in his head; then because of some creaking sound, made perhaps by a mouse in the wall, he had got up, feeling ashamed, and made his way on upstairs.

Now he went up to the very top, opened the door with his key, and began to undress, looking out at the hundreds of red roofs spread out in tiers in the morning sunlight.

# Seven

The bars of the iron bedstead were black, and the same shape as the backs of the chairs on the Champs-Elysées or the Bois de Boulogne. Désiré slept under a sloping attic roof. The skylight stood open. Birds were bickering along the ledge, and trucks from far afield were rattling past in the streets below, converging on the flower market; the sounds traveled so clearly through the thin air that one could almost smell the stacks of mimosa and carnations.

Désiré was almost immediately engulfed in sleep; he would first feel himself drop vertically, as though sucked down by an eddy, but it was not unpleasant, he felt no fear, he knew he would not touch bottom; like a cork, he rose up again, not quite surfacing but sinking and rising again, and almost always the same thing went on for hours, slow or sudden alternations between the glaucous emptiness of the depths and that invisible surface above which the world went on living.

The light was the same as that which pervades sheltered coves of the Mediterranean; it was sunlight, he realized, but sunlight diluted, diffused, sometimes broken as though in a prism, suddenly violet, for instance, or green, the intense green of the legendary, elusive green ray.

Noises reached him as they must reach fishes

through water, noises perceived not with the ear but with the whole of one's being, absorbed and assimilated until their meaning may perhaps be completely altered.

The hotel remained silent for a long time, because all those who lived there were nocturnal people; but there was a vicious creature over the way, a car that was taken out of a garage at the same time every morning and washed at the edge of the sidewalk under a spattering hose, after which the engine would be started up. This always required several attempts. He would wait tensely until the hoarse roar became a normal tone, and then for several minutes, he never knew how many, there was a sustained hum with a reek of gasoline fumes that must be blue-tinged. And meanwhile, presumably, the chauffeur, in his peaked cap and dazzling white shirt sleeves, was calmly polishing the chromium while the creature warmed up.

There was a streetcar which always seemed to get out of hand and run into the curb at exactly the same place, probably at a bend in the street.

When he sank deeper down the sounds became different, the images lost their clarity, even their separate identity; for instance, probably when a woman was washing herself in the attic next to his, at about eleven o'clock, he heard the splash of a fountain in the garden of his parents' country place at Le Vésinet, where, as a child, he had slept with the windows open during the holidays. He could clearly see the fountain, the wet dark stone, but there was something else he could not recall, the smell of the air; he tried to remember what the air of that holiday home was like—honeysuckle, maybe?

He would rise up, light as a bubble, and pause just before breaking the invisible surface; he knew nonetheless that the sunlight was cutting his hinged skylight in two, that it was just about to reach the foot of the bed, that he could dive down again, that the game was not up yet. . . .

That morning, as on other mornings, his eyes were smarting, he had the raw sensitive skin common to those who do not sleep at night, the lips particularly, which had the exquisite tenderness of a healing wound. He had gone to bed and let himself be caught up in the eddy, unresisting; he had sunk down, but had come up again immediately, he had surfaced, he had stared—so his eyes must have been open—at the whitewashed wall against which his overcoat, hanging from a yellow wooden knob, formed a black patch.

Why did he let this Empress business worry him? He closed his eyes, he dived, he did his best, but his impetus was feeble, he could not recover the wonderfully elastic fluidity of his morning slumbers, and unconsciously he stared at his overcoat, thinking of that Empress whom he could clearly recall, with her black eyes and hair; he was searching for a likeness; it bothered him, there was a likeness, he knew, it was in the eyes; he made a violent effort and discovered that, surprisingly and improbably, the Empress reminded him of his second wife, from whom he had run away.

The one was as lean as an umbrella and the other huge and flabby, but that was unimportant. It was in the eyes. That fixed stare. That unconscious, immense, haughty contempt, that apparent obliviousness to anything outside herself, anything unconnected with herself.

He turned over heavily on his hard bed, which smelled of sweat. He had grown used to the smell of his own sweat again, just as when he had been a child. For too many years, for the greater part of his life, he had forgotten the smells of which people who go about their business are no longer conscious; and he wondered if that were not the reason why . . .

He was close to a truth, a discovery, he had begun to dive down again, then something brought him back to the surface and he thought: "I won't go."

What was the good? What could he do?

He remembered her look of distress, her childish "Oh!" when he took her for the first time, clumsily, because he felt ashamed. And each time after that, each time they had sex together, though he tried to be as gentle as possible, he knew she was wearing the same expression, he avoided seeing her face, and thus it happened that instead of being a pleasure the sexual act became an ordeal.

He found himself sitting up in bed again. He said no, tried to lie down again, and a few minutes later he had thrust his bare legs out of bed and was hunting for his limp socks on the floor.

He was quite surprised to see that it was ten o'clock

already. Because of this, the panorama of rooftops had an unfamiliar look. He started to shave. Then, as he let one of his shoes drop, somebody knocked against the wall: a call to order from his neighbor, a croupier at the Casino who had a big blue-black mustache.

He went downstairs. In the ground-floor passage he met the maid who had stolen his money and had looked at him with hostility ever since. He said good morning to her with exaggerated friendliness, to which she responded with a curt nod while she mopped the tiles with a damp cloth.

He walked on as far as the Plaza, but before going in, as his mouth felt dry, he went into a bar for a cup of coffee. The hotel was a creamy-white building with a great many windows surrounded with ornaments, like a cake. He wondered whether the porter would let him in. Actually, the people who called at this time of day were chiefly tradesmen and workmen. The lobby was vast and cool. He went up to the concierge's desk.

"I'm from the Monico," he hurriedly said, as the other, who had a telephone receiver clamped to his ear, looked him up and down.

"Hello? . . . Yes . . . They're coming by car? . . . About two o'clock? . . . Good . . . Thank you . . ." Then, to Désiré: "What is it?"

"The boss would like to know what's become of the lady who was with the Empress."

A childish, ridiculous, useless lie.

"Madame Thérèse?"

So she hadn't changed her Christian name! She had become Madame Thérèse, just as he had become Monsieur Désiré. But his name was one picked up at random from a shop front.

"Is she still here?"

"No . . . I don't even know where you'll find her. . . . They've been pretty tough with her. . . ."

"Who?"

"Not the police . . . The police realized that she was just someone who had to earn her living. . . . Poor woman. She seemed so gentle. . . . You must have seen her, at the Monico. I know the detective from Paris went there last night. . . . Nothing, I suppose?"

"Nothing . . ."

"If I'd been here, I'd have called you up to warn you, just in case . . . When I heard about it I blasted the night porter, who hadn't thought of doing so. . . . You never know. . . ."

"Thank you very much. I'll tell the boss. . . . And what about Madame Thérèse?"

"They questioned her for three hours at least. . . . Then they had some food sent up for her, because she was exhausted. I don't know what the detective decided to do about her. . . . He informed the family—the Empress's family, I mean, for she's got a brother who's in the car business in Paris. . . . He's the French representative of an American make. . . ."

The concierge greeted a slim Englishwoman in a tailor-made suit, who was walking briskly past behind Désiré.

"A letter for you, Miss . . ."

He watched her move away. The revolving door sent a patch of sunlight sliding down the wall.

"As I was saying, they let the brother know. . . . He immediately telephoned instructions to a local lawyer . . . Less than an hour later, some legal people turned up and insisted on having seals put on everything. . . . The senior floor waiter, who'd been in the apartment several times to serve them drinks, told me it was a queer sight. They were terrified of the least thing disappearing. . . . They'd pick up every little thing, stockings, handkerchiefs, an odd slipper, and put them all away in cupboards and seal them up. . . .

"Apparently these people insisted on the police searching Madame Thérèse and they'd have sealed her up too if they could. It was all on account of the jewels, you see! . . . Seems they're all real . . . There were such a lot of them I'd have sworn they were glass beads. . . . It'd have been a major disaster if Madame Thérèse had taken any little thing!

"Why, that telephone call, just as you came in, was to tell me the brother is coming here by car presently, with a lawyer. They're on the road now, driving hell for leather. . . .

"Hello? . . . No, she's not here yet. . . . What's that? . . . Yes, she's still got her apartment, but she hasn't come in yet. . . ."

Since he looked on Désiré as a colleague, he explained, though without specifying to whom he was referring: "There's another queer customer for you!

She never comes in before eleven in the morning and she stays in bed till ten at night. . . . You wanted to know what's become of Madame Thérèse? . . . I don't know. . . . When they were through with their formalities they turned her out, there's no other word for it, without letting her take away anything, not even her personal possessions, which are all sealed up with the rest. . . . She had only her little handbag. She'd been crying. . . . I can still picture her on the sidewalk. . . . You could see she didn't know where to go, and she was like a stray animal. . . . In the end she went off toward Place Masséna. . . . If you're not anxious to meet the detective you'd better not hang around, because he's due here at eleven o'clock. . . . I don't know where they took the body. . . . It was taken away last night, but by the back entrance. . . . Apparently it's to be sent to America. . . ."

Désiré, too, lingered outside for a moment like a stray animal, and as his first wife had done, he made his way toward Place Masséna. He cast his eyes mechanically over the café terraces where, as yet, only a few people sat under the awnings, but he had little hope of seeing Thérèse there.

She must have taken refuge in a cheap lodging-house, in one of those squalid hotels in the old part of town where the washing hangs across the street and where small girls with bare bottoms sit on the doorsteps.

He crossed the flower market, where they were already sweeping up armfuls of flower stalks and buds, withered petals whose scent reminded him of All Saints' Day.

Had he any chance of finding her again? He scarcely hoped to do so, and he didn't know if he wanted to. And yet one does meet people one has not expected to see, since on a narrow sidewalk he brushed up against the Inspector, who was hurrying along, presumably to keep his eleven o'clock appointment at the Plaza, and who looked back, trying to remember, then went on his way.

Had he, too, gone in search of Thérèse? Probably not. He must know where she was.

Désiré went on walking. Then at midday he found himself back on Place Masséna, and he sat on the terrace of a large café where most of the tables were crowded with people drinking apéritifs. News vendors were calling out the names of foreign papers. Buses full of tourists in summer dresses stopped, then started off again, with rows of heads all turned the same way and all wearing the same smug expression of satisfied curiosity.

It was then that suddenly, amid the crowd, he caught sight of Thérèse. He almost lost her again, such was his astonishment. She was standing at the edge of the sidewalk, waiting for the policeman to halt the flow of traffic. He had to pay for his drink. The waiter, busy inside, was slow in coming. Monsieur Désiré knocked on the window with a coin. He was overcome with anguish, and yet he was incapable of leaving without paying.

The policeman lowered his club. The waiter came along, bearing a small tray which he proceeded to unload at the neighboring tables, pacifying his impatient customer with a "Coming . . ."

The pedestrians poured across. The stream dwindled, there was only one stout man belatedly hurrying as the policeman raised his club again.

"Haven't you any change?"

"It doesn't matter."

Too late. He had to wait. He tried to see her in the shadow of the chestnut trees along the boulevard; once he caught a glimpse of her light gray figure.

When at last he was able to cross he dashed forward, jostling passers-by, almost breaking into a run, and at last, some fifty yards ahead, he saw her again, walking slowly along, like a person who is going nowhere in particular and pretending to look at the shopwindows.

He slowed down. He had made no plan. He did not know what he wanted to do. He walked more and more slowly; they were only ten yards, then five yards, apart and she knew nothing about it, she seemed weary, maybe she was looking for somewhere to eat? The ridiculous thing was that finally she stopped in front of a window displaying pipes, and as he drew level with her, lacking the courage to go on this way with averted head, he called out automatically: "Thérèse!"

She gave a start, and turned around, frowning. The expression was so characteristic of her and of nobody else that the years seemed to vanish and he recognized her completely, just as he had known her: a frail, defenseless little creature, petrified with fear at the slightest noise, aware of the impossibility of flight and standing motionless with head drawn back, watching with gentle, astonished eyes as the cruel world swoops down on it.

He recognized the whole thing so vividly that his throat felt constricted and for a moment his eyes were dimmed and he saw her less distinctly. The clarity of his vision was restored just as Thérèse, who had been feverishly searching her memory, discovered the truth at last and revealed her astonishment.

She could hardly believe, as yet, that this was not some fresh trap, and she seemed on the verge of flight. She stammered out: "It's you!"

What did he say to her? He did not know. They were in the sunlit street; the shadows of the plane-tree leaves formed a quivering pattern on the paving. People were hurrying past. Cars glided by, a couple of yards from them. He looked at all the pipes in the window, and he spoke to her:

"I knew you were in Nice. . . . Don't be afraid. . . . I know all about it. . . ."

Amazement widened her mauve eyes. For they were really mauve. Monsieur Monde wondered whether they had always been that color. True, the lids were coated with eye-shadow that left minute glittering particles. Under her chin the skin was streaked with fine wrinkles.

What could her thoughts be on seeing him again? Was she listening to what he was saying?

"I'll explain to you. We ought to go and sit somewhere first. . . . I bet you haven't had any lunch. . . ."

"No . . ."

The "no" did not refer to lunch; it was a protest, a
feeble refusal of her whole being, with a shake of the
head. Perhaps she thought it was not possible? Perhaps
she was denying the reality of their meeting?

"Come along. . . ."

She followed him. He walked too fast. He had to
wait for her. It had always been like that when they
walked together. He seemed to be towing her along,
and when she was exhausted she would beg for mercy,
or else she would stop without saying a word to get back
her breath, and he would understand.

"I'm sorry. . . ."

Only, soon after, he was off again without realizing
it.

At the corner of a street there was a little restaurant
with a few tables outside; one of these, beside a green
potted plant, was free.

"Let's sit down here."

And he thought: "Luckily, we've got the street, the
passers-by, the waiter coming to ask what we're going
to eat and to straighten the glasses on the table.
Luckily, there's always something outside ourselves,
we're never left face to face. . . ."

"Give us the menu . . . anything will do. . . ."

"Will you have shellfish?"

"All right . . ."

"There's *brandade de morue. . . .*"

He suddenly remembered that she disliked salt cod and he said no. She was looking at him, still in amazement, and had only just begun to see him as he really was. Their situations were dissimilar. He, for his part, had had the opportunity to watch her for hours through the spy-hole at the Monico. She must have been surprised, above all, by the way he was dressed, for since becoming Monsieur Désiré he had gone back to the ready-made suit he had bought in Paris.

"What do you do?"

"I'll explain. . . . It's not important."

"Are you living in Nice?"

"Yes. I've been here some time. . . ."

It would take too long to tell, and it wasn't interesting. He was beginning to regret having shown himself to her. This was not what he had intended. He had only wanted to know where she was living, so as to send her a little money. For he had his earnings. And he still had some money left of what he'd had in his wallet at the time of the theft.

She was even more ill at ease than he. She had almost addressed him as *vous.* The *tu* had come to her lips nonetheless, and they felt almost as if they were standing naked in front of one another.

"Here we are, *messieurs-dames.* . . . And what wine?"

He was suddenly reminded of another restaurant, of that three-story eating place at Marseilles, by the rose-pink of the shrimps, the yellowish-gray of the clams, and the aroma of the wine that was being set before them.

What a journey he had been on since leaving Paris! He kept on touching the table to make contact with reality. And Thérèse, with her painted, aging lips, asked hesitantly: "Have you been very unhappy?"

"No . . . I don't know. . . . I didn't understand. . . ."

She seemed even more astonished, and her eyes, a little girl's eyes in an aging woman's face with flaking skin, opened wider in ingenuous questioning.

Did he understand now? That was probably what she meant. It wasn't possible. And yet he was a different man. He, too, had faded. His cheeks had the flabbiness that comes from a sudden loss of weight. His waistcoat hung loosely over his stomach.

"Eat up," he said.

Did he know that she was hungry, that since last night she had been homeless and penniless? It was not obvious. Her light coat was uncrumpled. She must have gone somewhere, perhaps to the Casino, where she was known, and maybe the barman had offered her something?

She went on eating. She was making an effort to eat slowly, with the tips of her lips. And then she said: "If you knew how it distresses me to meet you, like this!"

So now she was sorry for him, she commiserated with him! Once again a tiny frown puckered her brow.

"How did it happen?"

He looked at her so intensely that he forgot to

answer. She added, shyly—she was almost afraid of being heard:

"Was it because of me?"

"No, no . . . It's nothing to worry about, I promise you. I'm quite happy. . . ."

"I thought you'd married again."

"Yes . . ."

"Your wife?"

"It was I who left her. It's of no importance. . . ."

And the waiter set before them a dish of tripe, succulent and strong-smelling. She was not struck by the incongruity, because she was hungry, but Monsieur Monde found it hard to swallow a mouthful.

"I've just had a misfortune, " she murmured as though to excuse her appetite.

"I know."

"How did you know?" Then, with a sudden illumination: "Do you have some connection with the police?"

He did not laugh, or even smile, at her mistake. It was true that in his drab clothes he looked rather like some humble auxiliary of the police.

"No . . . All the same, I know about the whole business. I've been looking for you all morning. . . ."

"For me?"

"I called at the Plaza. . . ."

She shuddered.

"They were so unkind," she admitted.

"Yes . . ."

"They treated me like a thief. . . ."

"I know. . . ."

"They took away all that I had in my bag and only left me a twenty-franc note. . . ."

"Where did you sleep?"

"Nowhere . . ."

He had made a mistake in speaking of that, for now distress was choking her and she could not eat.

"Have a drink!"

"I'm still wondering what you do here. . . ."

"I'm working. I was tired of my life."

"Poor Norbert . . ."

He froze, suddenly. She should not have spoken so, in that foolishly pitying tone. He gave her a hard, resentful stare. They had barely been together a quarter of an hour, half an hour at most, and she had already degraded everything to the level of her own feminine mind.

"Eat up!" he ordered her.

Oh, he was well aware of her thoughts. Unconsciously she was, once more, putting herself at the hub of things. If she wore that guilty look, it was because she was convinced that she was responsible for everything.

And in her heart of hearts, for all her airs of distress, she must have been enjoying her triumph.

It was she, of course, who had caused him such distress when she left him! And although he had married again and sought to make a new home for himself, he had never found happiness again!

He would have liked to make her stop talking. He would have liked to go away now, leaving her the wherewithal to feed herself and keep going somehow.

"Was she unkind to you?"

There was unkindness in his own sharp retort: "No!"

"How you said that!"

And a heavy silence fell between them, while she went on eating, without enjoyment or appetite.

"Waiter," he called.

"Monsieur?"

"Coffee, please."

"No dessert?"

"For Madame, but not for me."

It was as though she had sullied something. She was so conscious of this that she stammered out: "Please forgive me. . . ."

"For what?"

"I've said something silly, haven't I? You were always scolding me for saying silly things. . . ."

"It doesn't matter. . . ."

"If you knew what a shock it gave me just now! . . . To see you like this! . . . In my case it's my own fault. . . . And then I'm used to it after all these years. . . . It's not the first time I've been in this fix. But you!"

"Stop talking about me."

"I'm sorry."

"I suppose the police are making you stay on in Nice?"

"How did you know? Yes, until they've finished their inquiry . . . and various formalities. . . ."

He took his wallet out of his pocket, and felt himself

blushing as he did so. Still, it couldn't be helped. He made sure that the waiter, stationed at the entrance of the restaurant, was not looking at them.

"You've got to find somewhere to stay. . . ."

"Norbert . . ."

"Take it. . . ."

Her lashes were wet with tears, but they were tears that did not flow, they rose to the surface but found no free outlet.

"You make me feel wretched. . . ."

"No, no . . . Careful, we're being seen. . . ."

She gave two or three sniffs and, in a gesture with which he was becoming familiar, raised her open handbag to eyelevel so as to repowder her face.

"Are you going to leave me already?"

He made no reply.

"Of course you've probably got your job. I daren't even ask you what you do. . . ."

"It doesn't matter. . . . Waiter!"

"Monsieur?"

"My bill . . ."

"Are you in a hurry?"

He was. His nerves were on edge. He felt that he might as easily be moved to anger as to pity. He needed to be alone again and above all not to have her in front of him, with her candid eyes, her wrinkled neck.

"Go and look for a room at once and get some rest."

"I will."

"When do you have to appear before the police?"

"Not till tomorrow. They're expecting the relatives. . . ."

"I know. . . ."

He rose. He had counted on her staying a little longer on the terrace, to finish drinking her coffee. That would give him time to get away. It would make things easier. But she rose too, and stood waiting beside him.

"Which direction are you going in?"

"Over there . . ."

Toward Place Masséna. Toward his hotel. For some unknown reason he did not want her to know where he lived.

Once more she trailed along behind him. He was walking fast. In the end she understood that it was no good persisting and she slowed down, like a runner giving up a race, but she had time to whisper:

"I'll let you go off. . . . Please forgive me. . . ."

Awkwardly, because he did not know how to go about it, he failed to say good-by to her. His temples throbbed as he walked away in the sunshine. He was conscious of behaving cruelly.

"Please forgive me. . . ."

This time, he felt sure, she intended no allusion to the past or to all the things for which he might have reproached her. It was to the immediate present that she was referring, to their failure to make contact, to her own inability to behave as he would have liked her to.

He waited until he was far off before he turned around. She had only gone a few steps and then halted, to keep herself in countenance, in front of a leather-goods shop.

People who went past could not know. She was just a very ordinary woman. And he was just a man in a hurry, on his way to work like any other.

He reached Gerly's Hotel and caught sight of Julie having lunch with Charlotte close to the open bay window. He could not get into the hotel without being seen and so he went through the brasserie.

"Been out already?" she asked without interrupting her meal.

The frown deepened on his forehead.

"Has something happened?"

He merely muttered: "I'm going to get some sleep. . . ."

"See you tonight?"

"Yes . . ."

Not until he was on his way up the dingy staircase did he grasp the meaning of her query. It disturbed him. Why had she asked him that? Was everything again in suspense?

He found the maid doing his room and he turned her out, almost rudely, contrary to his usual manner. He lay down and closed his eyes in a rage, but nothing was as it should be, neither the shadows nor the light, nor the sounds, not even the twittering sparrows, and his whole being tossed impatiently in the drab limbo.

# Eight

Gambling was the opium of these people. Through his spy-hole Désiré could see them arriving, one after the other. First the croupiers, the sleek black ministrants of the rite, the professionals, who hurried through the hall without glancing around and made straight for the "workshop." They did not leave coats or hats in the cloakroom; they had their own closet in the holy of holies, their soap and towels, and often a pair of clean cuffs as well.

Then came the clients, some of whom were important citizens. When they pushed open the door of the dance hall they had already discarded their outdoor garments, so that they seemed to be quite at home. The waiters, instead of rushing forward to show them to a table, greeted them as old acquaintances. Almost all of them wandered about with the casual air of people who have not yet decided what they are going to do. They would go up and shake hands with Monsieur René, exchange a few words with him, and smooth their hair with a careless gesture.

Monsieur Monde was well aware, by now, that they were inwardly in a ferment. He knew them all. The first to arrive that evening was a big orange importer who, so it was said, had begun by selling newspapers in the street or shining shoes on the Rambla of Barcelona, and who, at the age of thirty-five, had millions to play with. He was as handsome and well groomed as a woman. All the hostesses in the club looked at him with longing or envy. He would smile to them, showing fine gleaming teeth. Sometimes between two games he would take a turn around the dance hall and order a few bottles of champagne for them, a sure sign that he had won; but he was not known to have any mistress.

There was also the mayor of a neighboring town, who always hurried through for fear of being seen. He was a lean, tortured creature. At the gaming table he had his own set of habits and superstitions.

There was only one woman, but she was regarded and treated as respectfully as a man; a woman of about fifty, who ran a fashionable lingerie store, and who never let a night pass without a session at the gaming table.

Many of them, almost all of them, looked like Monsieur Monde's former self. Their bodies were well cared for, their skins rosy, their chins smooth-shaven, they were dressed in fine-quality cloth and beautifully fitting shoes, and they were all mature enough to be people of importance, often indeed to be overburdened with responsibilities. They had offices, employees, workmen; or else they were lawyers or doctors with a wealthy and large clientele. All of them had homes, wives, and families. And all of them, every night, at a certain almost mystic moment, were irresistibly drawn from their chairs, as though under a spell. Nothing could hold them back.

In all probability some of them told lies, inventing some fresh alibi for themselves every evening, some new professional or social engagement.

Others failed to avoid scenes and reproaches, the wrath and contempt of wives who could not understand them, and these would slink in furtively, ashamed of their presence here, ashamed of themselves.

None of them knew that behind a little round spy-hole a man like themselves was watching them.

There remained the suckers, the simpletons, the braggarts, the foreigners brought in by touts as though on a leading string, who were made to drink at one of the tables before being gently propelled toward the "workshop" for a game that was more or less rigged.

And finally those who did not gamble, for whom gambling held no attraction, who took the dance hall and its crowd of women seriously and spent hours there stimulating their sexual appetites.

Monsieur Monde could see them, a hundred times in the course of an evening, leaning over toward their chance companion, Julie, Charlotte, or another, and he knew exactly what they were saying—just a couple of words: "Let's go. . . ."

And the girls would answer, tirelessly and with unvarying innocence:

"Not right now . . . The boss wouldn't let me leave yet. . . . He's very strict. . . . We're under contract. . . ."

They had to go on drinking. Bottles of champagne

succeeded one another, flowers, boxes of chocolates, fruit. The whole thing was rigged. And when the time came at last, when dawn was near, sometimes when the sun had risen, the man, dead drunk, was thrust outside; very occasionally, the woman would accompany him to his hotel, where because he had drunk too much he was unable to perform.

Monsieur Monde, that evening, was thinking about them and about himself, meanwhile making a note of the bottles that left the pantry. He was thinking, too, about Thérèse. He had slept badly that afternoon. Afterward he had gone back to the restaurant where they had lunched together. Since they had made no plan to meet again, this was the only place where he might possibly find her. It had struck him that she might come back here, following the same line of argument as himself. He had questioned the waiter, who, however, had already forgotten her.

"A lady in a white hat, wasn't it?"

No such thing. It didn't matter. Besides, did he really want to see her again?

He felt tired. He felt old.

Monsieur René was, as usual, propped up on one corner of the table eating something. The busboy pushed open the swinging door. He made no announcement, merely summoned the dance-floor superintendent with a jerk of his head.

Monsieur René drew himself up at once and darted, quite unruffled, into the hall. The busboy hurried him to the main entrance. Just as he reached it, the door opened; and Monsieur Monde saw Thérèse herself appear. And Thérèse was quite obviously no longer welcome at the Monico. Monsieur René, without appearing to do so, was blocking her way. She was talking to him. She looked humble. He was shaking his head. What could she be asking him?

Monsieur René was moving forward gradually to make her retrace her steps through the door, but she outwitted his maneuver. The hostesses, who had understood that something was happening and who perhaps guessed what it was, were all looking curiously in that direction.

Thérèse went on imploring; then she changed her tone, uttered threats, insisted on coming in, wanted to speak to somebody else.

This time the man from Martinique laid a hand on her shoulder. She shook him off, and Désiré pressed his face closer to the spy-hole.

What could she be shouting at him with such vehemence? And why did the waiters, of their own accord, move forward strategically in support of their boss? How could they have guessed what was going to happen?

Suddenly, in fact, just as Monsieur René was slowly pushing her away with both hands, Thérèse drew herself up and began to scream, her body tense, her face unrecognizable, presumably hurling coarse insults or threats at him.

Désiré could not tell how it had happened, but there she was on the floor, literally writhing in a wild fit of hysterics; the others, the *maître d'hôtel* in black and the waiters in their white aprons, bent down quite unmoved, picked her up, and carried her out, while the music went on imperturbably.

Monsieur Monde looked at Julie and saw that she was unconcerned. A waiter, whom he had not heard come into the pantry, sighed philosophically:

"She may as well go and have her fit on the sidewalk. She's bound to finish the night in the police station. . . ."

"What fit?"

"She's run out of morphine. . . ."

Then he slid off his high stool, abandoned his so-called desk, and made his way to the squalid back stairs. Halfway down he began to hurry, for he had to go a roundabout way to reach the main entrance. From a distance, in the darkness, he could see two or three of the Monico staff in the doorway, watching a retreating figure that kept stopping and turning around to shake a fist at them and hurl fresh insults.

He took his former wife by the arm. She gave a start, not recognizing him at first, and tried to struggle. Then she saw his face and burst into dreadful laughter.

"What do *you* want? . . . So you followed me, did you? . . . You're even more of a bastard than the rest!"

"Be quiet, Thérèse!"

He could see figures at the corner of the street. People were coming toward them. They might be policemen.

"Of course, I've got to keep quiet. . . . You paid for

my lunch! . . . I ought to be grateful to you! . . . And you gave me some money. . . . Say it, why don't you? You gave me some money! . . . But you took care to leave me stranded in the street. For the rest, you couldn't care less."

He held on to her arm, and was surprised to find such strength in it. She kept on struggling, escaping from him, starting to run, and he would catch up with her, and she would turn on him and spit in his face.

"Leave me alone, I tell you! . . . I'll find some. . . . I've got to find some. . . . Or else . . ."

"Thérèse!"

"You beast!"

"Thérèse!"

Her face was distorted, her eyes were wild. He saw her collapse on the sidewalk at his feet, scrabbling at the pavement with her nails.

"Listen, Thérèse, I know what you want. Come along. . . ."

She did not hear him. The people who had come around the corner passed close by them and stopped for a moment. A woman was muttering: "It's shocking!"

Another, rather older woman was saying to the two men who were with them: "Come on. . . ." And they went, regretfully.

"Get up . . . Follow me . . . I promise you . . ."

"Have you got some?"

"I haven't, but I'll find some. . . ."

"You're lying!"

"I swear to you . . ."

She was laughing hysterically and looking at him wide-eyed, torn between mistrust and hope.

"What'll you give me?"

"Morphine."

"Who told you?"

She struggled to her feet, unconsciously using her hands like a child. She was swaying and weeping.

"Where are you going to take me?"

"To my place."

"Where's that? Are you sure you're not going to take me to the hospital? They did that to me once before. . . . I'd be capable of . . ."

"No, no . . . Come along. . . ."

"Is it far? . . . Let's go and find some morphine together."

"No. When you're calmer . . . I give you my word of honor I'll bring you some. . . ."

It was grotesque, tragic, and ugly: at times the scene would lose some of its intensity as Thérèse grew calmer, and they would walk a little way past the houses, like ordinary passers-by; then she would stop again as though she were drunk, forgetting what he had just told her and clinging to him. Once her weight nearly dragged him to the ground.

"Come along. . . ."

They made a little headway. And they both ended by uttering incoherent words.

"I went everywhere. . . . I went to the doctor that *she* got it from. . . ."

"Yes, of course. Come along. . . ."

"They gave *her* as much as she wanted, because of her money. . . ."

"Yes, yes . . ."

Twice he was on the point of leaving her there and walking off. The journey seemed interminable. At last they saw the lights of Gerly's Hotel, and then there was a fresh scene when he tried to make her go in.

"I want to wait for you in the café. . . ."

"No . . . Come up to my room."

He managed it, by dint of patience. He had never imagined life could be so tedious. He went up behind her, pushing her. She was in his room at last, but her suspicions revived, and he realized that she would try to escape; he went out swiftly and locked the door behind him.

Pressing his ear to it, he spoke to her under his breath.

"Stay quiet. Don't make a noise. In less than a quarter of an hour I'll be back and I'll bring you some. . . ."

Was she exhausted? He heard her collapse onto the bed, where she lay moaning like an animal.

Then he went down. In the brasserie he went straight to the manager and spoke to him in low tones. But the manager shook his head. No. He didn't have any. They didn't go in for that sort of thing. It was dangerous. You had to be very careful.

"Where, then?"

He didn't know that either. Cocaine and heroin were

easier to get. He had heard of a doctor, but he didn't know his name or address.

Monsieur Monde was determined to leave no stone unturned. He didn't care what people might think of him. There was one doctor who came to the Monico almost every evening, played for high stakes, and often left again looking pale and distraught. He, perhaps, might understand.

The hardest part, for one who was only a member of the staff, would be to make his way into the "workshop" and get close to the gaming table. Still, it couldn't be helped; he would go.

Then the manager of the brasserie raised his head. "Listen!"

In spite of the six floors that separated them from the attic, they could hear a noise. It came from the stairs. The two men hurried up. The higher they went, the more clearly they could hear someone banging on a door, screams, the voices of a maid and of a lodger who happened to be at home and who was questioning the frantic woman.

"You shouldn't have brought her here," the manager sighed.

What could Monsieur Monde do? He was at his wits' end.

"Call a doctor, will you? . . . Any doctor will do. We can't let this go on. . . ."

"Do you really want it?"

He nodded, thrust aside the maid and the lodger,

and fitted his key into the lock. They wanted to come in with him, but he disliked the thought of anyone else witnessing the scene, and slipped into his attic, closing the door behind him.

The quarter of an hour that he then spent, alone with the woman who had once had such innocent eyes and who had borne him two children, was something about which he never spoke afterward, and of which perhaps he managed to stop thinking.

The lodger, a jazz musician who had been confined to his room for a few days with pleurisy, had gone back to bed. Only the maid lingered on the landing. She was relieved when at last she heard the doctor's footsteps on the stairs.

When the latter opened the door, Thérèse was lying across the bed with her legs hanging down. Désiré was stretched half across her, pinning her down with his weight and holding her mouth shut with his hand, from which the blood was streaming.

He was in such a dazed condition that for a moment he could not understand what the doctor had come for, and stayed there in his strange position.

Then he got up, rubbed his hand over his eyes, and swayed. For fear of fainting, he went to lean against the wall, and the whitewash left marks all over one side of his suit.

The doctor had offered to take her to a hospital, but he had refused. The others could not understand why.

One injection had quieted her. She lay with her eyes wide open. But she was so calm, with such a vacant look, that she seemed to be sleeping.

On the landing he had had a whispered conversation with the doctor.

And now the two of them were alone together. He had sat down on a chair. Sometimes he felt a great hammering inside his head and at other times a dizziness, as though a sort of vacuum were sucking him down and preventing him from thinking. Now and then he would say mechanically, as though speaking were a relief to him: "Go to sleep. . . ."

He had switched off the electric lamp, but the moonbeams were streaming in through the open skylight and it was in that cold light that he saw her, transfigured; he tried to avert his eyes, because she looked like a dead woman, with the same pinched nostrils that the dead have, the same unsubstantial quality.

Once when he glanced toward the bed a shudder ran through him, because he seemed to see there not Thérèse but his son Alain, who had almost the same features, and in any case the same pale eyes and waxen complexion.

People were returning to the hotel. Their footsteps almost always stopped on the lower floors. He automatically counted the landings. Four . . . Five . . . This time they came on, up to the sixth floor. A woman's. There was a knock on the door.

He realized that it was Julie.

"Come in. . . ."

She was taken aback by the darkness, the strange look of these two creatures, the woman prostrate and open-eyed, the man sitting on a chair and holding his head in his hands. She began, in an undertone: "Is she . . ."

She dared not finish.

"Is she dead?"

He shook his head and rose wearily. Now he'd have to explain things. My God, how complicated it all was!

He drew her to the door and onto the landing.

"Who is she? Did you know her? I heard, at the Monico . . . The boss is furious. . . ."

He disregarded this.

"You knew her, didn't you?"

He nodded. And she promptly guessed something further.

"Your wife?"

"My first wife . . ."

She showed no surprise, rather the reverse. It looked as if she had always suspected something of the sort.

"What are you going to do?"

"I don't know. . . ."

"Tomorrow you'll have to start all over again . . . We know her sort. . . ."

"Yes."

"Who gave you some?"

"The doctor . . ."

"When the time comes she'll want some more. . . ."

"I know. . . . He's left me an ampule."

It was extraordinary. Words, phrases, even facts themselves—realities, in short—had lost all importance for him now. He was lucid and he was aware of it, he knew he was giving rational answers to all her questions, and behaving like a normal man. At the same time he felt very far away, or rather very high up; he could see Julie in her evening dress, on the landing, under the dusty electric-light bulb, he could see himself with ruffled hair and open-necked shirt.

"You're bleeding. . . ."

"It's nothing. . . ."

"She did it, didn't she?"

Yes, of course! All this was unimportant. In the last few hours, perhaps in the last few minutes, for he didn't know quite when it had happened, he had taken such a prodigious leap that he could look down with cold lucidity on the man and woman whispering, on a hotel landing, shortly before daybreak.

He was certainly not a disembodied spirit. He was still Monsieur Monde, or Désiré, more likely Désiré. . . . No! It didn't matter. . . . He was a man who, for a long time, had endured the human condition without being conscious of it, as others endure an illness of which they are unaware. He had always been a man living among other men and like them he had struggled, jostling amid the crowd, now feebly and now resolutely, without knowing whither he was going.

And now, in the moonlight, he suddenly saw life

differently, as though with the aid of some miraculous X-ray.

Everything that had counted previously, the whole integument and flesh and the outward appearance of it all, had ceased to exist, and what there was in their place . . .

But there! It wasn't worth talking about it to Julie or to anyone else. And in any case it wasn't possible. The thing was *incommunicable*.

"Is there anything you need?" she was asking. "Wouldn't you like me to have some coffee sent up?"

No . . . Yes . . . He did not care. On the whole, no, so that he could be left in peace.

"You'll let me know how things are going?"

He promised. She only half believed him. Perhaps she expected to discover, when she woke at midday, that he had gone away with the woman now lying on the iron bedstead?

"Well, cheer up!"

She went off, regretfully. She would have liked to communicate something to him herself, to tell him . . . what, exactly? That she had realized from the start that it wasn't for ever. That she was just a common girl but that she could guess how things were; that . . .

He saw her, at the bend in the staircase, looking up at him again. He went back into the bedroom and closed the door; he had a shock on hearing a voice mumble faintly: "Who was that?"

"A girl I know . . ."

"She's your . . ."

"No . . . just a friend."

Thérèse reverted to staring at the sloping ceiling. He sat on his chair again. From time to time he raised his handkerchief to wipe the blood from his hand, which she had bitten deeply.

"Did he leave you any more?" she asked again without moving, speaking in the hollow voice of a sleep-walker.

"Yes."

"How much?"

"One."

"Give it to me now. . . ."

"Not yet . . ."

She resigned herself, like a little girl. And in her present state she seemed far more childish and yet far older than when he had seen her in town the day before. His own face, too, when he lingered for a quarter of an hour in front of his mirror, shaving, often seemed to him like that of a child grown old. Is a man ever anything more than that? You talk of the years as though they existed. Then you notice that between the moment when you still went to school, even between the moment when your mother tucked you up in bed, and the moment you're living through now . . .

The moon was still shining faintly in the sky when the dark blue of night yielded to the light blue of morning, and the bedroom walls took on a less livid, less inhuman whiteness.

"You're not asleep?" she asked again.

"Not now."

"I do so want to sleep!"

Her poor weary eyelids were fluttering, she was clearly on the verge of tears; she was far thinner than she used to be, an old woman with barely anything left of her body.

"Listen, Norbert. . . ."

He got up and went to splash his face with water, making a noise on purpose to prevent her from speaking. It was better so.

"Won't you listen to me?"

"What's the use?"

"Are you angry with me?"

"No. Try to sleep. . . ."

"If you'd give me the second ampule . . ."

"No. Not before nine o'clock."

"What time is it now?"

He looked for his watch, which he had laid down somewhere, and was some time finding it.

"Half past five . . ."

"All right . . ."

She waited, resignedly. He did not know what to do or where to go. He tried to distract himself by listening to the familiar sounds of the hotel, where he knew nearly all the lodgers. He could tell who had come in, he recognized voices that reached him only as faint murmurs.

"It would be better to let me die. . . ."

The doctor had warned him. A short while ago—the doctor was still there—she had played the same trick on them, but then it had been on an impulse; at the height of her hysteria she had seized a pair of scissors that were lying about and tried to cut her wrists.

Now she was trying it again, deliberately, and he was unmoved. She persisted: "Why won't you let me die?"

"Go to sleep!"

"You know I can't sleep like this."

There was nothing to be done about it. He went with a sigh to lean against the attic window, from which he could see his red roofs once again and hear the noises from the flower market starting up. This was the moment when his night watchman on Rue Montorgueil, in his little cubbyhole, would be warming up his morning coffee in a small blue enameled coffeepot and drinking it out of a peasant bowl with a pattern of big flowers. Les Halles would be in full swing now.

And for years, at a somewhat later hour, in a double bed on Rue Ballu, he had wakened of his own accord, invariably at the same time, and slipped noiselessly out of the bed, leaving a lean, hard-featured woman lying there. While he washed and dressed with meticulous care, as he did everything else, an alarm clock would sound over his head and the tall youth who was his son would yawn and get up, with his hair on end and a sour taste in his mouth.

Had his daughter made it up with her stepmother, now that he was no longer there? Probably not. And when she was short of money she had no one to turn to. It was strange. She had two children. Presumably she loved them, as all mothers do—or was that all a fairy tale?—and yet she lived without bothering about them, often staying out late at night with her husband.

It was the first time since his escape that he had thought about them so clearly. Indeed, he could hardly be said to have thought of them at all.

He felt no pity for them. . . . He was quite cool. He saw them one and all as they really were. He saw them far better than before, when he used to meet them almost every day.

He had ceased to feel indignant.

"What are you thinking about?"

"Nothing . . ."

"I'm thirsty. . . ."

"Shall I get you some coffee?"

"Yes, please."

He went downstairs, in his slippers, with his shirt still unbuttoned over his chest. The brasserie was closed. He had to go outside. At the end of the street he caught a glimpse of the sea. He made his way to a small bar.

"Would you give me a small pot of coffee and a cup? I'll bring them back presently."

"Is it for Gerly's?"

They were used to this in the neighborhood. People from Gerly's were always fetching things at the most unexpected time of day.

On the counter there were some hot croissants in a basket, and he ate one and drank a cup of coffee, gazing vaguely into the street, and finally carried off, for Thérèse, the small pot, a cup, two pieces of sugar in his pocket, and some croissants.

Early-morning people met him and turned back to stare at one who was so obviously a nocturnal creature. A streetcar passed.

He climbed up to his attic again and guessed that Thérèse had been up. Perhaps she had hurriedly got back into bed on hearing his step on the stairs?

She was no longer quite the same. She had a fresher look, perhaps because she had powdered her face, touched up the delicate pink of her cheeks and painted her thin lips afresh. She was sitting up in bed with a pillow behind her back.

She gave him a wan, grateful smile and he promptly understood. He put the coffee and croissants on the chair, within her reach.

"How kind you are . . ." she said.

He was not kind. She followed him with her gaze. They were both thinking of the same thing. She was scared. He opened the drawer of the bedside table and, as he expected, the ampule was not to be seen. The syringe was there, fitted up and still wet.

With a pleading look, she stammered out: "Don't be cross with me. . . ."

He was not cross with her. He was not *even* cross with her. And a few minutes later, as she was drinking her coffee, he caught sight of the empty ampule gleaming on the sloping roof, just below the attic window.

# Nine

Leaving Nice proved as simple as leaving Paris. There was no conflict, there was practically no decision to be made.

About ten o'clock Monsieur Monde closed his door quietly and went down four flights to knock gently on Julie's door. He had to knock several times. A sleepy voice asked sulkily: "Who's there?"

"It's me."

He heard her coming, barefooted, to open the door. Then, without even a glance at him, her eyelids half glued together, she hurried back to the warmth of her bed. But though almost asleep again, she asked him (and her face reflected her effort to keep on the surface): "What did you want?"

"I'd have liked you to stay up there for a while. I have to go out."

Julie, struggling against sleep, breathed good-naturedly: "Wait a minute. . . ."

This was the last time, he knew, that he would be in her room, breathing its intimate atmosphere, its cheap pungent scents. The bed was warm. As usual, her underclothes lay in a heap on the rug.

"Hand me a glass of water. . . ."

The toothbrush glass would do. She sat up, asking as though in a dream:

"Anything wrong?"

"It's all right. She's asleep. Only I think it'd be better not to leave her alone."

"All right. Should I get dressed?"

"It doesn't matter."

She put on no underclothes, no stockings or panties. She merely slipped a short woolen dress over her body, and thrust her bare feet into high-heeled shoes. However, she peered into the mirror to powder her shiny face and put on some rouge, and passed a comb through her hair.

"What am I to tell her if she wakes up?"

"That I'm coming back."

She went up the stairs, docile and indifferent, while he went down and entered the brasserie. This morning he was not wearing his drab, night-worker's suit, but the more elegant outfit, the flannel trousers and double-breasted blue jacket that Julie had made him buy on the first day.

He had a call put through to Paris and went to wait for it in the brasserie where the proprietor was doing his accounts.

"Are you leaving?"

It seemed self-evident to him, as it had to Julie.

The telephone conversation was a long one. At the end of the line Doctor Boucard uttered profuse and interminable exclamations. Monsieur Monde, who knew that he was rather scatterbrained, repeated each of his injunctions several times.

Then he made his way to the shop where he had

bought the suit he was now wearing. He found another, more formal, more suitable for Monsieur Monde, and they promised to have the alterations finished by the afternoon.

When he returned to the hotel he found the two women sitting amicably on the bed together. They fell silent as he came in. Curiously enough, Julie's expression had now become more respectful and more subdued.

"Am I to get dressed?" Thérèse asked almost gaily. And she added, pouting: "Couldn't we all three have lunch together?"

It was all of little consequence now. He acquiesced to all their whims, including the choice of a rather luxurious restaurant and a somewhat oversplendid menu. From time to time Thérèse's eyes betrayed anxiety and her features grew tense. At last she asked him, tremblingly:

"Could you get any?"

He had some in his pocket and, with their coffee, he slipped her an ampule; she knew what he held in his closed hand, took her bag, and rushed off to the toilet.

Julie gazed after her and stated with conviction: "She's lucky!"

"Oh?"

"If you knew how happy she is! The things she said about you this morning . . ."

He neither smiled nor frowned. At Gerly's Hotel a money order, telegraphed by Boucard, awaited him. Leaving the two women together again, he went back to the tailor's and then to the station to reserve his seats. The train left at eight o'clock. Julie, at the station, was torn between laughter and tears.

"Funny how it makes me feel," she said. "Will you think of me from time to time?"

Monsieur Monde and Thérèse got on the train, had a meal in the dining car, and then went off to their compartment in the sleeping car.

"You'll give me another tonight, won't you?"

He went out into the corridor so as not to see the gesture that he anticipated, the sharp, almost professional jab of the needle into the thigh. He still mistrusted her, and gave her the top berth. He himself slept very little, and kept waking with a start.

He was very calm and clearheaded. He had thought of everything. He had even informed the Superintendent, before he left, that he was taking Thérèse to Paris.

At the station a new morning, a new town awaited them, and Doctor Boucard was waving to them from the end of the platform.

Monsieur Monde and Thérèse walked the length of the train, jostled by other travelers. She dared not cling to his arm. She was surprised to see that someone had come to meet them.

"Will you excuse me for a moment?"

He watched her out of the corner of his eye while he exchanged a few words with his friend, who could not conceal his amazement.

"Come here, Thérèse. Let me introduce one of my very good friends, Doctor Boucard."

She looked suspicious.

"Let's get out of this crowd first. . . ."

Once outside, he sought a taxi and made her get in; the doctor followed.

"I'll see you presently. You can trust him. He's not taking you where you might suppose."

The taxi moved away just as Thérèse began to struggle, protesting loudly at her betrayal.

"Don't be afraid," Boucard said with some embarrassment. "Norbert telephoned me to rent a comfortable apartment for you. I was lucky enough to find one right away, in Passy. You'll be at home; you'll be quite free. I think you'll have *everything* you want. . . ."

Thérèse's pointed features expressed surprise mingled with a kind of fury.

"Did he promise you anything different?"

"No . . ."

"What did he tell you?"

"Nothing , . . I don't know. . . ."

She bit her lips, vexed with herself for having been so stupid. Only a short while before, in the train, when the smell of Paris was already in the air, she had laid a hand on Monde's arm and had been on the point of bursting into tears, perhaps of prostrating herself in gratitude. They had been standing in the corridor and only the arrival of a fellow traveler had prevented her from doing so.

"I'm such a fool!" she spat out in a tone of contempt.

For she had believed that it was for her sake that he was coming back!

At ten o'clock Monsieur Monde, before making his way to Rue Ballu, got out of his taxi near Les Halles and walked the short distance to Rue Montorgueil. The weather was dull this morning. Perhaps it had been dull in Paris all the time he had been in the South? The absence of sunlight only made things sharper and clearer. Their outlines showed up starkly.

A truck came out of the shed, and he stepped back to let it pass. He went into the covered courtyard, turned left, and entered the office that he used to share with Monsieur Lorisse. The latter, overcome with emotion, began trembling and repeating in an excited stutter: "Monsieur Norbert! . . . Monsieur Norbert! . . ." Then, suddenly embarrassed, he introduced a personage whom Monsieur Monde had not noticed and who was sitting at his own desk.

"Monsieur Dubourdieu . . . An administrator whom the bank . . ."

"I understand."

"If you knew in what a fix . . ."

He listened. He looked. The whole thing, including Lorisse, including the administrator in his funereal black, made him think of a stiffly posed photograph. He went out of the room in the middle of their conversation, leaving the astonished Lorisse with his sentence unfinished, and made his way to the other offices.

When he reached the last of the row, he looked through the glazed door and saw his son. The boy happened to look up, saw him too, opened his mouth, and sprang up.

As he opened the door Monsieur Monde saw him turn pale, sway, and topple over. By the time he stood at his son's side, the boy was stretched out on the dusty floor and they were slapping his hands to revive him.

Later on, in the lunch break, two clerks who had witnessed the scene discussed it with a warehouseman, and one of them asserted, almost indignantly:

"He didn't turn a hair. He was completely unmoved. He just looked him up and down and waited for him to come to. You'd almost have said he was annoyed about it. When the kid opened his eyes and stood up at last, in fear and trembling, the boss merely gave him a kiss on the forehead and said: 'Good morning, son!' A man that everyone had believed dead for the past three months and more!"

However, when Monsieur Monde went for lunch at his usual restaurant in Les Halles, his son was his sole companion. He had not telephoned to Rue Ballu, and he had forbidden Monsieur Lorisse to do so.

"So you really believed I'd never come back? . . . How's your sister?"

"I see her from time to time, secretly. Things are

going very badly. They're up to their ears in debt and they're suing mother."

Alain seemed reluctant to meet his eyes, yet Monsieur Monde had the feeling that in time he would succeed in making friends with his son. At one point he involuntarily fixed his gaze on the lace-edged handkerchief, and the boy noticed this and blushed. A few minutes later he left the room to visit the toilet, and when he returned the handkerchief had disappeared.

"I don't know very much about it, but I think all the trouble was about the safe. . . ."

"Your mother had the key. . . ."

"Apparently that's not enough. . . ."

Monsieur Monde wasted no time. By three o'clock he was with his bank manager. At five, and not before, he stepped out of a taxi in front of the house on Rue Ballu. The concierge gave vent to exclamations. Monsieur Monde, however, was simply coming home, not even like a returning traveler, since he had no luggage; he just rang and went in, as he had done every day for years and years.

"Is madame up there?"

"She's just gone out in the car. I heard her giving Joseph the address of her lawyer."

Nothing had changed. On the staircase he met the maid—his wife's personal maid—who gave such a start that she nearly dropped the tray she was carrying.

"Look here, Rosalie . . ."

"Yes, monsieur?"

"I don't want you to telephone to madame."

"But, monsieur . . ."

"I tell you I don't want you to telephone to madame. That's all!"

"Has monsieur had a good journey?"

"Very good."

"Madame's going to be . . ."

He did not listen to any more, but went up into his own room, where with evident satisfaction he put on one of his own jackets. Then he went down into his study, the old study with the stained-glass windows that had been his father's and his grandfather's.

Nothing was obviously changed there, and yet he knit his brows. He tried to find out what was wrong. Then he saw that the ash tray was missing from the desk, as were the two pipes which he smoked only in private, in this room. In their place he saw a pair of spectacles, his wife's, and on the blotter a file of unfamiliar business papers.

He rang, and handed it all to Rosalie.

"Take these up to madame's room."

"Yes, monsieur."

"Do you know where my pipes are?"

"I think they've been put away in the bottom of the bureau."

"Thank you."

He was trying out the room, as one might try out a new suit of clothes, or rather, as one tries oneself out in a suit one has not worn for a long time. Not once did he look at himself in the glass. On the other hand, he went to press his face against the windowpane, in his usual place, and beheld once again the same bit of sidewalk below him, the same windows across the way. At one of these, on the third floor, a little old woman who hadn't left her room for many years was staring at him through her curtains.

He had just lit a pipe, and the smoke was drifting cozily through the room, when he recognized the sound of his own car drawing up in front of the house, and the creak of the door as Joseph opened it.

At the same moment the telephone bell rang and he lifted the receiver.

"Hello? Yes, speaking . . . What? . . . Did it go all right? . . . Poor woman! I expected that. . . ."

Steps on the stair. The door opened. He saw his wife framed in the doorway. But he went on listening to Boucard.

"Yes, yes, she'll get used to it. . . . No, I won't go. . . . What's that? . . . What's the use? . . . So long as she's got what she needs . . ."

Madame Monde stood there motionless. He looked at her calmly and saw her little black eyes lose some of their hardness, and betray, possibly for the first time, a certain confusion.

"Right . . . Tomorrow . . . See you tomorrow, Paul. . . . Thanks . . . Yes, yes . . . Thank you!"

He hung up, quite calmly. His wife came forward. Her throat was so constricted that she could scarcely speak.

"You've come back," she said.

"As you see."

"If you knew how I've suffered . . ."

She was sniffling, and wondering whether she ought to fling herself into his arms. He merely brushed her forehead with his lips and clasped both her wrists for a second, in an affectionate gesture.

She had noticed everything, he was well aware: the pipes and the ash tray, the absence of the spectacles and the file. She felt impelled to remark: "You haven't changed."

He replied, with that composure which he had brought back with him, and under which could be glimpsed a terrifying abyss: "Yes, I have."

That was all. He was relaxed. He was part of life, as flexible and fluid as life itself.

Without irony, he went on to say: "I know you had some trouble about the safe. I'm very sorry. I never thought for one moment about that formula which I've signed so many times: *I certify that my spouse . . .*'"

"Don't say it!" she begged.

"Why not? I'm alive, as you see. I shall presumably have to go and make a statement to that effect before the police, whom you must have notified of my disappearance. . . ."

He spoke of it without a trace of embarrassment or shame. He said no more, however, gave no explanation.

Every week, or almost, Julie would write to him on notepaper with a letterhead from Gerly's or the

Monico. She gave him news of Monsieur René, of Charlotte, of all his acquaintances. And he would answer her.

Boucard, meanwhile, talked to him every evening at the Cintra about Thérèse, who longed to see him again.

"You ought to go there once, at least."

"What's the use?"

"Just imagine, she believed that it was for her sake that you . . ."

Monsieur Monde looked him quite calmly in the eyes. "And so?"

"She was dreadfully disappointed."

"Oh."

And Boucard desisted, probably because like everyone else he was deeply impressed by this man who had laid all ghosts, who had lost all shadows, and who stared you in the eyes with cold serenity.